I0527420

THE SIGNATORY

KIRK MARSHALL

SKYLIGHT PRESS

© Kirk Marshall, 2012

First published in Great Britain in 2012 by Skylight Press,
210 Brooklyn Road, Cheltenham, Glos GL51 8EA

Cover artwork by Liberty Browne
Designed and typeset by Rebsie Fairholm
Publisher: Daniel Staniforth

www.skylightpress.co.uk

Printed and bound in Great Britain by Lightning Source, Milton Keynes.

British Library Cataloguing in Publication Data.
A catalogue record for this book is available from the British Library.

ISBN 978-1-908011-41-1

This book is for Andrew Marshall,
Bearded Briton and bird-watching dilettante,
For educating me in the wonders of the flock

For a moment the two of them looked at each other, wordless, as if they were asleep and their dreams had converged on common ground, a place where sound was alien. – Roberto Bolaño

I am a moat-maker. How I came to be a moat-maker (which was not my intended profession, but a consequence of my dispassion with it), how I was witness to the death of my sharpest friend – sharp, for his demise cut me with a singular brutality unlike any equitable loss – and how this all conspired to befall me in Scotland, where men and goats are frequently confused for one another by the undiscriminating eye, has little to do with the linearity of reason, and more to do with the legend of a swan, a disastrous letter, and the fruits of a parentage that I'm steadfast in describing, in my mother's own elegant terms, as a "tiny bit too ramshackle for most".

It began, with the rapid collapse of my summer of promise after my newest girlfriend cuckolded me, when I received a phone call from my dazzling and freakish friend, Adolfo Cavaggio, an Italian:

'Sebastian, it has been too long. You must come and purify yourself by ingesting five litres of uncultured dry wine with me and awakening to locate a tattoo in, how you say, the deepest cleft of your anus. What is your answer?'

I contorted my body to disentangle the picket of kinks that had marshalled immediately to bedevil the phone-cord, all the while persevering with our unforeseen conversation in between an arrogant and dissolute effort on my part to light a cigarette on the heel of my shoe.

This vaudeville fiasco devolved into an uninsightful event in which I was compelled to accept responsibility for loafing the underside of my honey-tallow Jack London suedes with nicotine, before I careened off-balance and kneaded the formica flooring with my face.

'Whoopsy-daisy!' I swore.

7

The whole time I maintained my clasp on the receiver, as though Adolfo's ironical generosity, his engaged presence on the end of the line, constituted a doting stewardship, a parental eye that mentored rather than hectored: but this assertion demands that I intervene and come clean by revealing that I've always been the casualty of idealistic, if not spiritual folly. There is nothing patriarchal nor prayerful about Adolfo: our friendship is a woe-fostered corollary to our romantic loathing for one another, for in he I discern the bastard I secretly yearn to actualise, and in me Adolfo identifies the simpering cock he recalls once inhabited the mirror a decade ago when seeking out his own reflection. We are broken versions of one another; we are a family of one. If either of us matured enough to cite disenchantment and claim a renewed distance from the other in totality, if either of us ever demonstrated the self-summoned solidarity to reject or defect from the other, we might ourselves locate only half a man: half a man, and double the rancorous twat.

Our co-dependency is a socially-incentivised device used to second-guess and keep in check our obscene dispassion with our lot in life. We are servicing our humanity with the most warped collegiality.

'I believe you mean the interior buttock, Adolfo! To be decent, I'm not really sure I'm seeking companionship or unwashed inking syringes in my arse at the moment. I've had far too brief a chance to exert my prowess in self-loathing throughout the week, and I fear I want to give it my best, old chap.'

'What are you talking about? You've had decades to refine this ambition! And to be perfectly lapidary, Sebastian, you've transcended most teeth-gnashing competitors. A credit to your miserable, damaged, collapsed-romantic heart.'

'Cheers, Adolfo. You're ever so endearing. Why is it we don't speak more frequently than once every eclipse?'

'Too many wolves in the phoneline these days, Sebastian. Can never be certain if molecular nanobots engineered for attraction to soundwaves are archiving our conversations as phonic data for future legal incrimination.'

To the sympathetic nostril of the worldly masses, this may have elicited a pungent tang of schizotypal paranoia, but Adolfo was the benefactor of a fair point: if a faction of our sterling British law-

8

enforcement agencies ever demonstrated the intellectual stamina to deploy an investigative eye into his affairs, it wouldn't take long for inquiries pertaining to his domestic plantation of nutrient-rich high-grade cannabis crop or the mechanism of his bootleg whiskey operation – distilled in his soak-in bathtub – to yield an acrimonious opposition to Adolfo's hazy lifestyle. Fortunately it was *he* who'd possessed or inherited the omniscient gaze of Sauron, even if said receptacle for sight was bloodshot not from piercing through the miasmic veil of Mordor but rather the discomforting reefer curtain of smoke luxuriating between the rooms of Adolfo's palace of squalor. No English police with their ear to the grindstone had cottoned on to the man's debauch – yet.

He was like Ralph Ellison's *Invisible Man* transposed to a Benny Hill reality involving sex-starved Scotland Yard bobbies. All they'd ever catch of his superior disrepute were the giggles of nude girls in rollerskates shepherding Adolfo away to newer plateaus of safety.

'So where's Pamela now, my golden kibbutz? I'm assuming she's cut her losses.'

'Ha ha,' I ventured, lingering in a state suspended somewhere between convalescence and suicide. I wanted to blubber and recite stylistically adventurous poetry down the phone, or at least a dirty limerick, involving my recently departed and bone-marrow syphilis, but my tearducts were intent on deviating from my higher assignations. Instead, they wished to twinkle in merry abandon. Fucking genealogy: it's not my fault I'm biologically subject to a case of chronic tear-constipation. My father was an evil bastard, and short of an opthamalogical transplant I would forever be burdened with his eyes as my inheritance.

'Pam fucked off, I dunno, maybe a week ago. I don't understand the logic of the human calendar any more, Adolfo, unfortunately. I've been communing with the cats.'

Adolfo paused, the unheralded pocket of silence alluding to the spectacular immensity of the tirade yet to squeeze through the pinholes in my receiver and lurch into the narrow yew-sheer confines of my ear canal. I could sense the vibrations in his breathing the way a dog can inhale a whiff of subatomic geosmin in the atmosphere and decide on that haunting evidence alone that a strident storm was about to befall the parched world proceeding unawares beneath.

9

I could hear the thunder booming in the dark somewhere, in the driest sanctum of his Italian septum.

'The trouble with women,' he sighed, with theatrical pulchritude, reminding me of a telemarketer who dreams of the stage, 'the *apex* of the female paradox, *amico mio*, is that the moment a woman decides to leave you is the preclusion to your relationship in which you live in a golden era, the time in which all love seems not merely possible but germane to survival. Of course, this is an entrapment devised by your woman to lure you into a false sense of comfort. It may only last a week, ten days max, but your relationship improves a thousandfold the moment the woman involved decides to soften the impending blow by treating your opinions and curiosities with a heightened degree of respect. It's like a suicide in that way, Sebastian, for a woman's mind equates approaching tragedy as a self-assumed certainty, and there can be no discomfort or anxiety over ambiguity in the conviction of a break-up. She will restore blood to your most vacant or injury-sustained interior, she will lighten the mood that may have stole over the threshold of your shared household and between your tasteless kisses, she will disperse the shadow from their throngs over your icy, damage-inflicted, toxically-entangled heart, she will convince you there is *passion* in raucous song within you both yet. *Then* she will inform you all this has been for nought – that it was a masterly performance conducted with smoke and mirrors. This will directly result in the dissolution of all impermanent ceasefire: she will make it known that in advancing moments you shall endure hell.'

He cleared his throat, obviously satisfied with the tenor and poise he'd channelled in which to deliver me this monologue. 'I believe you are experiencing firsthand that particular romantic punishment, the one society associates with fire and immaculate torment. Now, Pamela has left you as a boorish husk, empty of all incentive, and without a redemptive erection in sight. Am I right?'

'That all seems pretty misogynistic in its articulation of the female engagement with heartbreak. I'm not sure I agree that it's all as calculated and opportunistic as that.'

'Well maybe I've been watching too many insect documentaries. The point is that Pamela probably hated you for a long time, and with much fiercer conviction, than you hope to muster or reciprocate. So instead, I want you to erase her, and her absurd, sublime, lust-igniting female contours from your deepest sense of self, and look to the benefits of travelling overseas with me, to chase down a different breed of bird altogether. Savvy?'

'Are you still rattling on about those nonsensical red swans? Dear Adolfo, when will you learn that there is neither dignity nor financial solvency in being crazy and anonymous? I'm afraid you're quite a psychotic when it comes to the business of mythological birdlife, which would be countervailed if you indulged a little less in recreational frivolity and invested more time in establishing your sadomasochistic porn kingdom like we all recognise you're capable of.'

'Are you in or are you out, Sebastian?'

'To be eminently clear, I do not miss Pam. She signifies little to me other than a bitch with an admirable sense of timing.'

'Fucking fit, though.'

'Alright, I'm in, by crook and by hook! I'll start packing, shall I? Where should we arrange to reconnoitre to discuss our scheme?'

'The airport. I'll book the tickets – doing so as we speak. We'll only secure time away from the jocular high society and plush livery of sweet-cheeked Mary England for three days, a week max. You deserve the adventure, after all the boiling brimstone. Oh, and Sebastian?'

'Mm?'

'What's your credit card number? I think I've forgotten the last four digits.'

A surly, gassy and indelicate glow of foreboding gripped me in a ghastly box-hold: I had succumbed to the charms of my old self once more. There's no experience quite equitable with the plight of a narcissist fearful of his inner desire.

I bided my time, in a haphazard mastering of nonchalance, for Adolfo Cavaggio at the baggage carousel while a mustering of babies shrieked for fear of flight or an exacerbated proximity with shrewd disconsolate bitches.

An airport such as Heathrow is a miraculous phytoplasm, an inverted virus in which quarantine is facilitated to keep the healthy and virile at bay: there's nothing worse than an airline passenger who *relishes* the packaged travel experience, for enthusiasm can be mistaken for agency, and the system recognises this. Far more *assuring* to clinicalise the threat of independent initiative with discounts on duty-free cologne decanted from the spleen of a semi-endangered primate, or to quell the possibility for immunised autonomy with glazed pastries that manifested the tortured configuration of a snail shitting out its weight in custard. Far more *discriminating* that an airport *leech you* of all expendable currency than air an artery with a transversal cut to the source of the blood sickness. After all, the flight industry wouldn't want to *cure* you of diagnosed consumer dependence. You might just freight over ocean to your intended travel destination by ship!

I'd been dispassionately test-driving this theory for its potential to be abbreviated into something resembling authentic wit, but my mouth was too invested in disagreeing with the nautilus masquerading as a breakfast croissant I'd just inhaled, and Adolfo's operatic materialisation quickly excelled in botching my risk-moiled venture at "departures-lounge philosophy". I abandoned the experiment before any lasting effects could be observed by naked flame.

I bugled Adolfo's approach with a brassy, pyrrhic fart to signpost this memory for future dispensation, and revelled in this most recent rendezvous by socking one of his world-famous ginger-gnarl ears with a swift fist.

'Howzit!'

He immediately collapsed to the floor, blood streaming from the protuberant gash. He was fierce with a blossomed levity, and his imperfect jackal grin was in full display. For a disquieted second, we were both startlingly welcome in each other's company.

Adolfo groaned in his own blood, down there on the carpet, for sport and companionship. I genuflected to his aid, producing restroom-dispensed paper serviettes to staunch the psychotic flow.

'Sorry about that, chap,' I contextualised, with a feeble sincerity. 'Didn't think you'd collapse like a baboon's decaying anus like you did. I do beg pardon.'

'Sebastian Fenugreek Sackworth,' Adolfo panted from the floor, spreadeagled and grinning with affectionate charm. 'You punched me in the head. May I remind you that this is a most uncommon greeting.' He paused, a frog-swarthy human folly in a rust-coloured suit and cheetah-print cravat like a fat person's topsail. 'It was most surprising. Well done.'

I inflated with the compliment. Unbeknownst to me, our surly greeting had coerced a coterie of sleep-parched lounge drifters to challenge both moral and pacifist inhibition and, with a disarming group-mind, coil around our badgered theatre of misdirected friendship with fervent eyes quickened by fear.

They wanted to know if Adolfo was capable of standing, and perhaps with a diminished sense of civic impartiality, whether I should be torn asunder, marrow from ligament.

It was a fundamental corollary of Adolfo's and my friendship that we famously attracted or determined looks of curious wrath wherever we conspired to greet each other within public proximity to the lowest common cultural denominators. I could not blame a duty-fevered London wage-worker from feeling compelled to, for example, dismantle a moulded plastic chair over my wizened spine, particularly at the sight of my pugilist descent into knuckleboxing an unsuspecting Italian photographer in the side of the jaw; it made sense that bliss-deviated onlookers might want to intervene on behalf of Adolfo's staggered regard for self-honour by taking me to the proverbial cleaners with a succession of taut caresses which the wittier of commandos are fond to describe as "etiquette enhancers".

I am just fortunate that when I am conscientious of the apparatus of an approaching arse-whupping I can frequently channel the penitent hangdog expression of a thirty-four-year-old wallflower beset upon by schoolyard memories of aspirating toilet water into my lungs whilst a foot levered my head further into the ceramic bowl of an unbleached student shitter: few agitated individuals are lacking in sufficient vanity, and overcompensating in the necessary and discreet conviction to combat crime in an airport such as Heathrow, especially when the perpetrator possesses a perfect symbiosis with runny turds, and the alleged victim is wheezing with tantric Italian laughter.

After all, you might accidentally dispense fisticuffs with a privileged twat, (like a heartbroken history archivist named Sebastian), and get foul shit all over your retracted slugging-fist. And who would want to risk *that* communal embarrassment?

'Wow, they really look as though their desire is to kill you, or storm to my aid,' Adolfo giggled, transferring the bloodied tumour of sodden paper serviettes into my whispering palm. 'And I don't mean a quick pack murder, either. Looks like they sincerely intend to extract your gonads through your feet.'

'Well they can all lope off and participate in carnal frustration with their least attractive second cousin, I'm afraid, because there's nothing further to entertain them here.'

I shook hands with my pain-softened companion, his scent abundant with citrus, Brighton lawns and hot vermouth. Adolfo, as so daring and irreparably was the case, exalted in an afternoon drunkenness that only remotely betrayed the absolution of my friend's radical depravity: he would always embark on the solvency and rapture of a new day in Leeds by guzzling Sardinian Sangiovese, red as aces, in a highball with his morning muesli and the weekend funnies. I wanted to strike a match off his face, I loved him so.

'C'mon then, let's monopolise ourselves a table,' he quarrelled merrily, with a belly-hazed temperament of sublime lethargy. 'I could really rape a long black.'

Our emotionally compromised rent-a-crowd overheard this and, bridling with the collective indignation of working-class hypocrites or reluctant racist sympathisers, dispersed to allow Adolfo and I to limp through the ruinous cathedral of Heathrow, his right arm slung around my accommodating shoulder.

'Psst! You can't say this sort of thing in the eavesdropping radius of passers-by,' I coached, with a gentle appeal to the scorn of our jostling neighbours. 'This is Great Britain, after all. You might scare the ethnicity-conscious holiday wallies back to the shires of Wimbledon, and then where would our economy be?'

The assaulted Italian favoured me with a wry, unassuming snort of the proboscis. 'Oh, psshaw. Save the colonising mission for Scotland,' he tousled, as we entered the electronic breezeway of the airport's open-plan café.

✡

The café was as close to an architectural test pattern as the broadcasting networks of reality had yet devised: the formica-top glazed basalt tables; the palm-sculpted stools bolted to the floor to best encapsulate the inertia of discomfort at being situated a distance of twenty centimetres too far from the counter-booth; the butt-clotted hollows of the ashtrays; the transparent tempered resin of the individual table-cloths metastasising with air pockets incapable of being deflated; the dessert menus offering a free waffle with everything like some griddle-latticed form of edible harassment; the clientele too enamoured with the thrill of international travel to concern themselves with the sterile space territorialised by the Ikea fixtures – or the mop and safety-cone collaborating to cleave the slick surface of the floor of an overnight vomit.

The girl behind the register was far too animated for someone limited to a vocational vocabulary of two conversation topics and desperate enough for a fortnightly paycheck that she wore a cap on her head advertising the airport's free waffle conundrum without visible cognitive conflict.

She was also prophetically attractive, as women always are in minimum wage airport shanties, and was probably studying for her Masters in Temporospatial Philosophy if her reverence for paid customer service indicated the vistas of her educational ambition.

I like to entertain the plausibility of a girl of this formula and sexual excellence – as striking as a fox in a greenhouse – exchanging robust banter with me from between the blaze of her bangs or the window of her fringe, but it is a consequence of my fidelity toward the competencies of narration that I explain my common misfortune with women: I style myself after Clark Gable, sporting a swale of pomade-scalloped hair bisected by a neat part and a turquoise tulip in my lapel, but my moustache is a relic from Edwardian poolhalls when "pencil-thin" evoked something other than claims of degeneracy, and my body is perhaps most acutely attributed as *pervertedly famished*, rather than elegant, which is not at all enhanced by argyle vests or hounds-tooth suits.

I am the regrettable lovechild of the Monopoly Man and Peter Doherty, with a face like a joint venture between a gargoyle and Fred Astaire, and I *am* hansom, like the cab: vintage enough to display an academic kind of novelty, but only really promising to women for a ride around the block or a rattle down the cobbles.

So instead of seductive parlance, the girl and I trade factoids about the culinary range of English muffins, whilst Adolfo coasts beside us, rehearsing dislocating his own jaw effectively enough to down the toasted foot-long focaccia being drawn and quartered at his expense.

'In Luxembourg, I believe, muffins are considered the flavour terminus of most communal meals. There is also a tendency for gourmet butchers to insert them up the buttocks of a roasted fowl or tenderloin as a form of golden-fried stuffing.'

These were all lies, of course, but the girl was indulging me at least until she discerned that I groped, with the depleted dexterity of all those for whom courtship was accomplished through no contribution of his own, for a punchline as intangible as a horizonline.

'So I'll have the one with the chocolate chips, please. I like the arse of my chicken to taste sweet,' I explained, until I realised what I'd announced aloud was increasingly dislocated from prior context, and the girl was surveying me as though conducting a census on the exact density of sweat flooding the pits of my arms and escaping, like a thief made from anti-freeze, down the back of my jean-clad calves.

'That was a joke, you understand.'

I cut a dramatic figure, whimpering before the muffin counter at an international airport.

Adolfo unsheathed a portion of the tart-hot vegetable focaccia from its foil-glossed cover-bag and massaged a steaming end into his mouth.

'Oh, I got it,' the girl assured me, her face as implacable as an Easter Island grotesque. 'Here's your muffin, Funnyman.' The paper bag, simpering from her fingertips, *limpid dead weight*, reminded me of something.

Adolfo and I swifted on our heels and located a cubicle vacated of all occupancy, save for the remnants of what might once have proven a magnanimous empire constructed obliquely from french fries, and I eased into an affectionate mode of finite contemplation as I gazed out the window.

Down on the tarmac, men in fluorescent safety jackets pursued tactical tracts to outfox the wind, which had mostly to do with avoiding being cannonaded into the propellers of a taxiing aircraft down on the runway, and forklifts burdened with misshapen boxes pixellated over the concrete like Tetris pieces dissolving between the two glass contours of a knuckle of bourbon.

I watched a nebula of what might have been orioles reach critical mass before exploding into a galactic halo-climb of perfectly geometric expression.

'You did well, there.' Adolfo was recovering from our earlier interlude of violence with apparent charm. He nodded at the counter. 'She was mere minutes away from asking you for your number, I'm sure, if only the button for airport security beneath her register hadn't converged with her index finger as inexplicably as it insisted in demonstrating.'

I shrugged, and liberated the muffin from its enclosure with a satisfying tear. I turned back to the window. 'What are they? Swallows?'

Adolfo dispatched a hand to his forehead and visored his eyes. He squinted against the sunlight, and yawned in leonine opulence from the divan of his reinforced-steel stoop. 'They're actually locusts. Your eyes just aren't accustomed to affiliating poetry with plagues yet. Never fear. Scotland will revise all that.'

I scoffed down a morsel of muffin, suppressing fleet and tenacious visions of the café girl transferring her tongue into the interior of my ear, and squared my elbows against the table's OH&S-flouting knife-sheer corners. I swallowed twice, the second time to pre-emptively discourage the rapidly accelerating possibility of my throat bursting with geysers of acid reflux, and commandeered a smile.

'Nice muffin?'

'Obviously.' I oscillated back to the window, and pointed with a belligerent commitment to science. 'You're the semi-professional ornithologist here, Adolfo, you've got to classify the birds for me. It'll speedily derange my fixation for taxonomy, otherwise. Might they be finches?'

Adolfo yawned once more, like a crocodile harbouring an orthodontic flock of ortolan, and grinned winkingly. 'They're common starlings, Sebastian. Note how they flush in almost algebraic synchronicity, how one pivoting in the opposite direction will automatically determine the new trajectory for the group, how the birds coalesce and atomise like the particles of a waveform, how change happens, with veracity, in complete *motion*.' He turned to me, and eclipsed one Italian palm in the other. 'That's how you achieve inner resolution: at the most svelte velocity. You don't get happy by loafing, Funnyman.'

'Subtle metaphor,' I muttered, bitter to the bastard dregs. 'I don't care that Pamela left. We didn't love each other. It just pulses, with that searching sort of pain, when you realise she was the clever one. She jumped ship before it sank. Now I'm floundering.' I appealed to my friend's semblance of earthiest compassion. 'I don't know what I'm doing. I mean, c'mon, fucking Scotland?'

He was tucking into his focaccia with startling savagery, but he managed to offer me a carnivorous smile abloom with charity, insight and roasted yellow capsicum.

'We find this swan, which I'm certain migrates in the spring to Kilmarnock, you maybe do some archaeological evidence-scouting for your university dissertation, we seethe in streams of froth and lager with the ginger natives, we find some penniless ladies who are willing to deplete our scrotums of all our mental woes, we gaze at some fireworks in the gutter of some socio-economically adrift idiot-county, comparing notes on our drug-detonated amnesia while writhing with fleas, we secure a mythopoeic status, and someone somewhere offers us kilts and cash if we fuck off home – it's all swimmily *graspable*. Scotland's the salve, Sebastian, Scotland's the answer.'

Adolfo lunged for my lapel, crushing the tulip in his fever. 'All we have to do is board our flight, flirt with the stewardesses for extra cashews, suppress our rampant fear of Gaelic faces or frost-stippled buttocks shorn of their flame-red eiderdown, prognosticate on a future which involves a land of milk and honeyed mutton, and graciously seize our deliverance not as bonglie exiles, but as wayfarer *dilettantes*! What could be interfering with your sense of adventure here? We're the remnants of a confederacy of libertines, Sebastian! The sun-vanquished vestige of this century's diminished aesthetes; this taciturn diuretic old nation's last surge of fire and shit!'

I disentangled his fingers from my collar with egregious restraint.

He looked gone, already lost to me, cracked and merled with a mottle of adrenaline and doom-fuelled lust. Before me sat Adolfo Cavaggio, some wild, ursine and holy-engulfed saint of unpopular risk.

18

I coughed into my fist. 'A last hurrah?'

'Yes! Yes, most explicit! By jingo, by crook, by golly gee willickers, the lad has it!'

I transferred my stare to the girl behind the counter, only now salient in my melancholy reservation to discern how much like Britain she resembled: so full of heat and time and the sweet valences of history, its darkest advance, bereft of interest in the druidic rants of two freaks of the sky, as she traded with me her severity through red hair and blue eyes.

I would not see her, nor my beloved city, again. It took one last pleading look from Adolfo to declare my intention.

'Alright, sweety. We've already booked the tickets, it's only fair. I'll do it,' I crowed, before punching him, stereoscopic and fierce, hard as I dare into his other ear.

There are few more transfixing vistas than being entitled to a vision of a glassy, membrane-clustered city of racing, pivotal electricity trembling in a white glister of night – a voyage of candles blurring the boundary between occupation and a desert of dark.

Scotland, it must be qualified, is no Tokyo; low to the latitude of the land, even sheep here glow like lanterns, and the contrived plot of streets courses through the still, stark narrative of wine-green haze, emitting light but little clarity.

What world awaits me I cannot apprehend or treadle with a confident act of navigation nor understanding, even though I submerge beneath the sleep-slack hoods to comb through red-eye enhanced memories of Mel Gibson being civically disembowelled on the silver screen, or Sean Connery sportingly exchanging glances and blows of a steel blade in a muster of Arthurian chainmail with someone who may have been either Kevin Costner or Richard Gere if there were some method of measurement beyond length of hair and depth of moral bankruptcy to differentiate them.

Scotland prevails in remaining beyond the apparatus of economy-class, brain-haunted speculation, and Adolfo is no more useful a seer in steeling me for our approaching landfall, despite his cackling mammalian protests that we're descending into the surly rectum of a new green future; if there was anyone more convinced that Scotland possessed the power to generate and manifest the cult of celebrity, it was my weird, box-eared fatuous Italian friend, dazed to his iguana gills with airline shots of vodka; delusions that the nation below us was civilised and less overthrown by disowned cats and boorish Australian scatpackers, and consumed by the rare distinction of a man obsessed with a legendary red swan.

His disappointment, from my adjacent mantle in the sky, was to be evident and visibly deflating, and I informed him of such. But the vodka had already wrought its corrosive, gullet-burning damage, because he merely winked at me, while we listed and veered toward the tarmac below us, his corpulent musical form addressing me with a fart that yearned for bagpipe accompaniment. Ah, the modern alarm clock.

It was a rinse of shock, watching the blazing smoke scatter to secede as Scotland swooped with its spires and steeples and weathervanes and neon billboards from out of the toll of sleep.

I made a joke about how planes accommodate similar emergencies by retrofitting each seat with a gas mask, and Adolfo grinned bright and veiled with pride before the stewardess complained that the cabin smelled of sour custard and heat-cooked jackjack fruit. Adolfo frowned immediately, and then we were tumbling through sea-peaked gusts, scarves warring on the airfield against our throats.

Wind reverberated in the eyelet of my navel like the howl of a sea-cave: Fuck me did I freeze.

✡

Adolfo and I assumed predatory configurations as we sliced through the armaments of the isle's wind-militarised defence, heads sheathed beneath hoods and our elegant clown-hewn dimensions rippling through the airport carpark.

I whimpered. Adolfo was palming the keys to our airline's agency rental vehicle – a suede-brown buffalo of a four-door sedan – covetously to his lusty Italian chest.

I conducted a perplexed reconnaissance of the clod-buffed hearse claiming occupancy of my dark, sleep-peopled periphery, and I yawned back a protest, not sure whether the car possessed the aptitude or trickery to metamorphose back into the roadkill yak that it clearly was.

'Well, Rum Punch, this is fucking smug,' I muttered, hurtling my luggage into the rear-boot, before observing to genuflect on the asphalt to loop up my shoelaces. 'The thing smells like a ruddy attic beneath a wheat-yard, and will be about as convenient to moor as a bleeding frigate, man.'

I fumbled my mobile phone from my pocket and switched it on with a gaunt apprehension that belied the concession to heartbreak I was struggling to portray. 'There's hardly any freaking reception. This is perfect bollocks.'

'She's not going to text you, Sebastian,' Adolfo glommed, flexing a swarthy eyebrow. 'Unless you're expecting requests for child support.' He shook his head. 'Here, put that away, before you get nostalgic delusions about fatherhood.'

I thrust the phone back into my jeans pocket and flared my nostrils, surveying the rental. 'Is this not the nearest thing to a turd on wheels you've ever seen?'

Adolfo blanched, affording me wide berth as he pursued tepid translations of my agitated behaviour from beneath a wary bloodshot gaze.

'There is a human surgical skeleton in the back,' he observes dryly, making flappy mouth-reflex exercises in the scarring, burn-bright wind of this blistering Scottish abandonment, as if spasming to divorce himself of a foul new taste. 'They did not promise the skeleton in the desktop literature, Sebastian. I'm certain no skeleton was referred to in the pamphlets provided prior to authorising payment for the rental.'

'You're spot on,' I coo, hands thrust in pockets, surveying the laboratory model of the human skeleton, its verisimilitude to the biological architecture of a death-softened human victim, all hinges and spines and harpsichord wreckage and reedy vertebrae. I cup my hand around the window glass and whistle for moral solvency, a mincing English lush alarmed beyond the laurel of hysteria at the horrible resolve that a skeleton is asprawl in his rental. I scurry for disgust, but am intercepted by a sense of admiration, tortured in its anatomy.

21

'I say, Adolfo, I think I rather like it.' I exchange the most whispered of fleet stares with the Italian, prior to engaging him with the rationale of my declaration.

A cigarette peeps from my tiny jarrah snap-case of smokes and lulls into my cushioned sneer: I light it with a shadowboxing stance, foisting the flame into the wind.

'The way I see it,' I drawl, taking a glossy drag, and surrendering to the welcome buzz of carcinogens thrashing off the walls of the bloodstream, long dormant of rain or heat. An awe, an ache, a muscle-mass of sub-zero scandal, one chain of wizard breath forges a passage through my veins. I stand and shiver, gratified for the bless of bad sensation. 'The way I see it is that this skeleton was forgotten by its owner, the previous recipient of the sedan; or else it was abandoned here to assume territory of the car by the rental company as a strategy to disorient and dispel the schemes of those who might wish to vault off with the vehicle.'

Adolfo narrows his eyes. 'Sebastian, who the fuck would want to steal this sedan?'

'Your point is not immaterial, I agree.' I inhaled another rose swarm of nicotine. 'But the predicament remains irresolute: a physician's skeletal mannequin lays nestled and brass-hustled into the corner of our backseat, and we do not possess a grasp on the lore of this malapropism in Scotland. Perhaps this is a commonplace highland greeting, a wholesome lark, a sly and gentle reception at our expense.'

I staggered the cigarette against my heel, embers wheeling from my extremities like a Peroclean saint. In a wink, the sparks were hints and whispers. 'I think we must embrace the hospitality.'

'Methinks the Scottish are demented in the fucking hindbrain,' Adolfo orates, his allegiances shifting beneath a slow, slaying grin. 'Not to mention the fucking forebrain and cerebral cortex,' he qualifies, before we sail into the scotch supple upholstery of our proud brown sedan, like balls into a well-parcelled oil-slack wicket-keeper's glove.

We fold into the chariot to accompany our inanimate passenger. 'We will have to give him a name,' Adolfo informs me.

✭

22

Oh no. Our foray into highlander road-veered jackanapes – with our car windows lashed shut to de-emphasise the authenticity or originary substance of our quest for excess – roaring in a quasi-convertible through the artery of the night, our heads bent low to honour the illusion of twilight sobriety, does not bode well for the incandescent sinew that is Scotland: we terrorise the twinkling swath of unconscious morning in our lurching-Blundstone boss of a brown jalopy, complete with skeleton companion and The Velvet Underground whirring, with scandalous power, through the grilles of the radio-set and via the fissures of my own human vehicle.

I am both spent and a little kinetic from having hit the sauce on the plane, but the velocity and lustre of night's own soapy black coat, like the pelt of a North Cumberland stag, bristles by leaving nought but an exfoliation of the soul; tired, but wired. Oh yes.

Adolfo and I exchange filterless paperback cigarettes, hoofing through hookah mouths the purple of tails from fading dragons, giggling to each other that we are old enough to be strafing and braving through the reckless tides of youth to commit ourselves to responsible living, but we are instead abusing this insight to glut on the milk husk of entropy, because sometimes a departure is less toxic, less formulaic than a return.

And Scotland unfolds her skirt.

We whoop, and I wrest down my window to drum the side of the jalopy with a display of superior cunning.

There is the fiercest might in us yet. We are in a new country after all, and because we are human and therefore crippled by a heritage of fear in the crest of the unknown, we set about claiming it for our mad tyranny. This involves roaring and parading your teeth, like a pair of chums flirting with cash before a casino slot-machine. Our total field of vision – that golden mean of witness – is hastily consumed by a howling waste of greenery. I retrieve my extremities and wind up the glass, spooked into reverence.

'It's everywhere!'

Neither I nor Adolfo nor our friend Vasquez Duchamp can swift our sockets or jolt the hinges of our unlocked jaws at a circumference of Scottish *terra firma* before us – the yawning pastoralia of an uncolonised plain – without it choking our lashes with the green of its advance, without it blinding our throats with the fury of its dereliction.

23

'Look at all the trees, man. This reminds me way too much of *Wolf Creek*.'

So this is *nature*, that bitch, at her most bestial, her least discreet: we are culturally-insensitive gits from England disinvested of mortal awe, for we hate the churlish perfection that the powers of the wild beyond summons for our tourist dispassion.

We both should feel obligated to revel in the majesty of primeval creation here, but all we can synthesise is a mutual sneer for the lush orchards that surround us. Scotland is a fucking dumpsite for wilderness. Where is the signpost for occupancy? Where are the symbols, the artefacts, the raw data to signify that this country complies to the prostitution and comforts of exploitation common to capitalist enterprise? We're not debating the conventions which govern semiotics here: this isn't a model for philosophy, just a panicked plea for the tiger balm of industry, suburban sprawl, gentrification, low-ozone pollution, the victory of clear-fell and roadside fast-food *chains* over those of DNA.

Christ if the virulence of the natural world didn't compel you to want to lash yourself fast to the nearest neon-warm wingspan of golden arches and refuse to submit to the environmental threat.

I would rue the day I retreated beneath the green peril, and so gnawing the inside of my cheek, croaked: 'It's a conservationist's wet dream, a consumer's weirdest nightmare.'

'Not even a conservationist would scorn the Colonel with so little remorse.'

And Adolfo was right, for the beatific gaze of the world's favourite deceased Yankee white supremacist was busily being cataracted by a virus of poison ivy as we drove past a billboard an hour out of town.

I said a heretical prayer, demanding the protection of the patron saint of Kentucky Fried Chicken down here on the human plane, but my heaviest and most pious words were carried away by the Scottish winds prowling by the carnage-green moors. We locked our doors and repented. We entrusted our surly brown jalopy to leave no evidence of our passing but our most generous carbon footprint, smoking Pall Malls until our skeleton friend shone yellow with clouds of pristine nicotine.

A house, small and fashioned from water, brick and mortar, now harangued the landscape. We trained the nose of our buffalo onto its distant taunt.

'Sebastian, surely the people who own such a property must digest the sweetest, purifying Starbucks coffee. We feast on sourdough rye, guffaw with the cast of Stephen Fry's *Q.I.* and sleep on Sainsbury linen tonight!'

We parked the car, after two hours of driving, and retreated into the wheezing cavity of Scottish corn and taro, hustling over a field as gold as a spillway of whisky.

We resembled the occupants of a Chagall painting as we cut forth in our advance: the flâneur and the red devil of Sicily, a pair of distorted souls lashed together by the sneery genius of entropy, a force which binds atoms the way intuitive timing yokes a punchline to a context.

Anyone distrustful enough to observe our raucous navigation through the blood of the field – orange now beneath the transfixed glow of the sun's staggered axis – might conclude that the noblest course of action involved our gun-snipered dispatch.

They would be right, of course – we were the human contagions of an incendiary illness called "decadent endangerment", because Adolfo was grunting for a miracle involving spontaneous alcoholic materialisation at this point, and I was palming a shaky trespass of bargain-bulk anti-depressants down my throat from the prescriptions he and I had earned through our remote emotions and psychosocial craziness – and we warranted gory blasts through our stomachs from the desperate and aghast warden of a peace-loving family of Scottish farmers at each passing second.

At any moment, at any angle, the shotgun bullets would come snaking through the tall grass. Exit wounds would yawn like bromeliads at sundown, torching tunnels through the fuselage of our muscle.

I clenched my eyes shut, suddenly startled by a molten lunacy which began raging through my veins, and I anticipated the violence that soon would befall us both, starving us of escape and deranged entertainment: detonating our entrails into the bitter tincture of Scottish afternoon. I lapped at my gloss of collected sweat, my pupils hunting the locus of the gentlest breeze, and yelped.

25

'Let's get the fuck out of here, man,' I parlayed, like the sworn enemy of the firing squad, 'there's something fucked about this field! Quickish now. Did you see that scene in the sequel to *Jurassic Park*? I swear there's sodding Velociraptors skulking on tooth and belly, just waiting to sail into the air with lantern smiles bristling full of teeth: I hate Scotland! This place is a snare to gobble innocent European travellers!'

I was hysterical at this point, shaking with a zeal to contend with Beyoncé and death adders alike. The drugs had finally triumphed over my wit-stripped, mash-scooped brain to seize sovereignty of my dwindling faculties and hollow out my thinking organ the way a wasp usurps a drone colony for a chance to taste the bonded floral sweetness of a honeycomb terrace: discard all the existing tissue and assume residence in the florets of my mind.

I was sure I was raving. It was the most fun I'd permitted myself to exalt in for a long time, at least as far back as feeding the corners of my toxic photographs of Pamela, pretty and cruel and viral and not really a flesh-perjured person at all but some extraterrestrial depression in the form of a leggy East Londoner, into the sear of my pocket lighter until all evidence of our romance rippled, distorted, buckled and burped into flame. Right now I'd recovered a familiar sense of sexy, joyful dread.

I howled into the brace of wind that swept up my sculpted hair.

I'm willing to suggest that it was probably an abstruse and fey design for me to appear more compromised by despair than a bitter indifference toward the accomplishments of theatre would ordinarily allow – it was a shaky call barren of pleasant behaviour which escaped my throat, my heart suddenly inhabited by wolves – but I couldn't channel the loathing for Adolfo's and my present predicament for long before even *I* found it an exercise in opulence.

There was no point exaggerating our Scottish isolation, for neither Adolfo nor an unseen butcher-man hankering for bloodshed in the tall grass would care to hear it: my inferiority of heroism was my own disability, and I would be the one to tolerate such a performance if it were to continue: I didn't possess much of a stamina for drama and alterity. So instead I hoiked up my lungs, and power-launched a concerning pearl of Cortez gold into the air, and it perched like a star-spangled yawn of light, as elliptical as a burning Venus, just for the fleetest of affairs.

And then it suffered internal collapse and showered the field with a fine mist of mucous.

'I'm sorry. I refuse to writhe in a scupper of fright over *this* fucking cornfield in Kilmarnock; now, my Italian Gargantua, disarming in both girth and gaiety, let us descend upon that quaint abode, before us, which approaches with a sharpish locomotion.'

I rotated to face Adolfo, who was now metres behind me, his face hot and awash with distress. He did not move. He merely stood, palms extended toward me in a gesture of submission and theological farce. 'Sebastian,' he swallowed.

And there *he* was: a dog-maned gunman, a face like a fall from grace, cosseted in a fold like a fist wrapped in wrath, standing but half a metre behind Adolfo with the barrel of a shotgun inserted between his shoulder-blades.

The highwayman snarled, and I realised late that it was a laugh.

'More cunts of the bonglie tribe, I see,' he'd offered, like a serenade fit to accompany the repeated kicks which might strike a cowering hound. 'We'll be needing introductions, innit, me dearies? Eh?'

This did not yield promise, so I said, 'My name is Sebastian Sackworth. You're here to impregnate our corpses, I presume?'

✡

There was nary a stir but the dropping of a mouse dropping.

The ears of corn funnelled in sound into a closed circuit, where even the chaff hissing in the blue-baled gust exhibited a bloodless impression of a clowder of mouths chewing tobacco. I could not isolate nor identify a finite rationale as to why Scotland should remind me of the Alabama swamp communities of the literature of Tennessee Williams, but I can confess that I anticipated at any second being sodomised by the butt of a rifle while entreated with a hemlock of favourite ditty chestnuts so profane that they, alone, would water the eyes.

It is perhaps reasonable to suggest that the infrequent comparison assumed between the Scots and the wily cackling hillbillies describing a lazy backstroke in lagoons of bootleg

27

moonshine familiar to Faulkner, is a negligence to discern the state of affairs that suggests modern ethnography has long excluded a possible relationship because of its obscene obviousness. You can't disqualify a Scot for being labelled a "redneck" simply because his pelt obscures a laboured study of the neck in question: never mind the flesh: dignify the blazing lustre of the hair for Chrissakes! I suppose what I'm championing here is accountability: there's no justice in *The Lonely Planet* failing to hint that a cultured English soul might be implicated to gird his loins when moving amongst the ginger natives of this colonial backwater.

Not for no reason am I instantly reminded of that iconic cinematic précis of all that Scotland has to endorse to the privileged world: an image of Ewan McGregor's Mark Renton exploding from the front-end of a shitter, glistening like a larva in a mucal membrane of human faeces and haphazard sewage; a Scot born to this world before our eyes, swaddled in the affluent cloth of effluent.

I now exchange daggers with Adolfo Cavaggio for the price of a counterfeit smile. But I will not retaliate with a sheepish denial.

'You fucking Italian pillock! Why the hell, for all that's unpolluted, did I allow you to convince me that *Scotland* would be an intelligent proposal! You obtuse Sardinian wanker!'

Adolfo cringed, like a disloyal daschund, and deployed a wobbly, recalcitrant eye toward our vocal accoster with the inventive dialect and orange teeth.

I feel, as any fearful and limb-buckled Englishman will in these frequent contexts where bloodshed is a pace or two from being wrought and one's nipples retract proportionately with the speedy discretion of bashful flying saucers, that I should supply here a concise overview of our attacker to better obstruct images of a pending violence populating my mind. (It's a remarkable phenomenon how effectively horror can be dismissed by investing one's focus on the *appearance* of said horror.) To illustrate such a maxim, I offer you the following statistics and definitional characteristics that apparently commingle to result in a Scottish thug, circa 2012.

Foremost is his face. To wit:

Our rifle-sculling agent of chaos and haphazard dentistry possesses a singularly exclusive one; it reminded me of the countenance of an otter if it had been carved into a pumpkin.

28

He possessed a tall, pendulous frame clothed in a flesh of tallowy complexion, with a whip of peppered hair no longer retaining an earlier earthier lustre, and a neck that gandered forth into the localised stratosphere leaving nought but the impression of an ostrich whose head – that sentient apex of all sophisticated multicellular creation – had been inflated to a size most alarming in its scorn for subtlety.

Our fat-headed aggressor resembled some monstrous doom-summoning face of spectacular tenderness dreamed up by Odilon Redon, adrift here above the whistling buds of Scottish pasture, irradiating a puzzled belligerence which spoke to me of secret satire.

He was, on closer inspection, also evidently not a Scot altogether, but an Icelander.

This, to me, warranted little consequence. He was about to gun me and my bosom brother down for afternoon sport (albeit I'm inclined to concede that there were certain familial inheritances that could be called into question inasmuch as siblings rarely result from the spermatozoa and fertilised eggs of distinct and unrelated parentage), but I wasn't about to succumb to epistemological fancies over the geopolitical identity of our man, this wannabe master of massacre: he could claim the flying isle of Laputa or Rangoon as the terminus of his birth – I cared not! – for still such cultural attribution would not distract me from the resounding threat of a live-action shoot-'em-up in which I was tormented by the contagion of his gun's scope-sight, soon to claim residence in the folds of my muscle and membrane.

To risk inelegance or to efface all eloquence I must render this explicit: my heart was now rippling like a flag accosted by a crosswind.

A squirt of hot piss ebbed down my leg, warping the shade of blue common to stonewash denim so that I now abandoned all dignity in order that I might comprehend the ephemeral material with which we fashion notions of human success: it all drowns beneath a soak of fear-incited urine, I'm afraid.

I bore my wet patch like a wound and a badge of honour, and I grimaced so as to console myself of embarrassment. (It works).

'I'm sorry. I don't imagine you could help us, there, my angry desperado? Forget all prior jest, for I was only responding in excitement at being confronted by the emblems of pending murder – which you must excuse – and permit me to inquire if you know the whereabouts of both a lavatory and a flock of rare birds?'

The Icelandic brute lowered his rifle, and transferred his gaze to Adolfo who was trembling like a rabbit cowering at the back of an open cage.

Our interlocutor seemed to hesitate for a moment – so arduous in its mounting possibility for further flirtation with the whispered sentiments common to an uncivil mutilation – and then his resolve appeared to collapse, for he welcomed us both with a gracious, coy smile.

He nodded. 'Dunno.'

'Aha. Do you think you could narrow the field?' I pressed on, relieved that discussion of ornithology could eclipse the relevance of illegal trespass with a flutter of an eager tongue. 'Perhaps you misunderstand. My associate and I are freelance journalists from abroad. He is a nature photographer, and has been commissioned by a London-based quarterly to present a story on the existence of a certain breed of red swan. You may have heard of the publication? It is known in global circles by the name *The Feathered Observer*, I believe.'

The Icelander offered up a waggish grin. I persevered.

'Daft title for a science periodical, I agree. I'm accompanying Adolfo as a research assistant. I'm currently enrolled in a PhD scholarship for the University of Kent in which I maintain the philosophical position that Anthropology promotes a historical method of taxonomy which is counter-intuitive to the preservation of landslide victims. This is merely a thesis for investigation which functions as an introduction to a discipline of specialised academia which I refer to as "Bog Studies". (This does not involve the intellectualisation of human poo, and its position of eminence as a fetish property, you understand.) So the reason we're here, at this precise junction in Kilmarnock, which you need not remind me is actually your field, and a splendid one it is that, is because our aspirations coalign with our desire to familiarise ourselves with the welter of Scottish peat dancing in our vision.

'Aha. To put blunt, I'm intent on conducting a little dig in the heath to search for evidence of human decay, while my compatriot

30

wishes to capture a dossier of photographic snaps which depicts the migratory behaviours of endangered birds in the wild. You therefore must agree that I harbour no particular ill will or contest with you, here, but merely aimed to approach your fine commode to inquire over local lore and directions.'

I swallowed, my head raging with the stark choir of doubts which assail an individual only moments preceding his unsung demise, and commandeered a futile grin. 'Of course, while I've been quaking in your fold of corn I've also been shitting myself like a jelly-bellied vindaloo virgin, which thus catalyses the riddle I must express concerning convenient lavatories.

'More specifically, is there anywhere I can take a dump in the privacy of my own teary breakdown while my bowel provides discourteous accompaniment in the form of a ripe and vivid solo? I would prefer some cool ceramic to cushion my cheeks, but I'm willing to rough it if you can indicate a good spot, while promising to avoid holding my companion at gunpoint. Otherwise you may have to claim ownership of a sudden and unforeseen plague of the "brown ninja", if you catch me. Obviously after such ablutions, I assure you we will both make ourselves scarce, as the expression goes, providing you give us a head's start before you see fit to punish our folly. How does the bargain strike you?'

I clamped my teeth together, the way a chimpanzee simulates cheer while advertising terminal fear: it was a beam devised by superficial light.

The Icelander's demeanour darkened at the conclusion to my soliloquy, and he scattered a blazing pair of blue eyes, like ice chiselled from sky, over Adolfo's and my delirious expressions of mercy.

His whole body sagged in an instant, like a man inside a monster suit at the opportune moment the children have departed. He seemed infinitely conflicted, and two suspicious eyes vaulted over the topography of hissing Scottish crop. Eventually a voice emerged, wholly unlike that which he'd originally entreated us.

'Beg pardon, one has to retain the act, keep up appearances, you see. Never know what unenlightened vagabond *sui generis*, is prime to interrupt my afternoon vigil. I was just out spotting, for I'm a keen birdwatcher myself. I believe by your remarks that you are

31

candidly making reference to the *Cygnus toro*, or tiger swan, said to be indigent to this region of Scottish moor-sedge and low-altitude marshland. You are, of course, aware that the species is ultimately mythical? And therefore impossible to view without first indulging in reckless and irrational voyages that may necessitate the sacrifice of civil decency?'

The Icelander gauged our unblinking and affectionable faces – slack with the telltale tailwind of hope stirring the brows – and then grunted his sober approval. The sunlight caught the calcium-barren roots of what must have once constituted blonde curls as gold as the wheat wuthering in bouquets by our waists, and the Icelander croaked a dark laugh that recalled the blooms of weird fungi in forsaken limestone caves far beneath a Scandinavian altar of ice.

'Then what is the genesis of our present hesitation, gentlemen? Come hither! Allow me to introduce you to my funky monkey.'

We played follow the leader, his shotgun cradled beneath the arm.

✸

His name was Ísleifur Reykjavík, an Icelandic attribution which, when unpacked, signified an "heir to the Bay of Smoke". This constituted a cunning and insightful *éponyme* to apply to the lamp-white, tremblingly narrow sprout of a soul now shepherding us both through the tussled tussock of the taro-wheat toward a wide and vascular plain in which all carp retreated before an unseen bulge of water.

'Only a little further,' he grunted, reminding me again why I don't trust strangers.

I watched the carp – their flesh mottled with the lithographic mysteries of the most agonising curatorial talent – describe sweeping arcs beneath the lavender malt of the surface. They thrashed and dipped, stalked and blimped through the salt stripes of the lake, occasionally clashing heads and swivelling the axis of their two-fanned flukes, turbulent S-curves bristling with a very intuitive, unintellectual fire, a sense of entitlement that could only be achieved through wrath. I offered both Adolfo and Ísleifur cigarettes from my jarrah snap-case, clasping it with an effortless scuttle of wood on wood before sheathing it back in the pocket suspended above my anus, and I ladled out a soup of exhaled smoke over the grade of the wet element, witness to a battle of fish against a creeping and intangible assailant.

'Man-made,' Ísleifur explained, pontificating around a breath of silver heat. 'It's an irreconcilably wicked irony of nature for the world to reclaim the land enslaved and distorted by man – sometimes within mere days of its construction. This reservoir was intended for the source of hydroelectric power from Kilmarnock which would guide renewable voltage to the furthest outskirts of our Scottish mire, but some industrialist naysayers stationed a few kilometres west of here and gratified with the fix they retained on the desalination plant chiming like clockwork out on the coast, decided to administer threats of a state-wide monopoly if work on the reservoir persevered. It was shut down in hours; the engineers and civic planners of the whole operation dispersed with the butter of commerce, tens of thousands in cash, fattening their pockets. Weeks later, the catchment was invaded by carp accessing the fish ladders affixed to the dam. As is evident, algae spawned in a canopy of green venom which polluted the waters and provided sanctuary for the carp, and the ecosystem was rapidly whittled to the bedrock until it yielded nought but a monoculture, a community of predators which ravaged and cannibalised the feeblest whitebait and even their own abundant parcels of eggs, so that no wildlife teemed below. It took a long time to live with: My gall at having been witness to an eyesore restored to the land, only metres shy of my own property line, in which no benefit would eventuate save the possibility of a health & safety hazard that would soon demand bricking over, only culminated in reassuring me the world was a barbarous place. I decided that I would gun down any future agent, representing the desalination plant in a power-suit, who trespassed my land. But then I was privy to a miracle.'

Ísleifur twisted his body to exchange an intimidatingly compassionate gaze with my own. His mouth contorted into a demilitarised smile of praise, of style. He appeared to be sublimating to some higher realm of perception before my eyes, where perhaps his appetite for snipering industrial turncoats in his wheatfield was reconciled, was sated by the nourishment of new wisdom. Perhaps not; heightened states of meditation don't diminish the value of a shotgun in the face of toothy, mandible-mouthed, sweet-talking commerce. He looked so vacant of internal contest in this second that it was like observing a tiger as it succumbs to a tranquiliser; the bitter fury of dwelling amongst dunces waning with the sweetest surrender.

'That's when I saw the swans,' he croaked.

Adolfo's ears rattled to attention; he could not have appeared any more alert to Ísleifur's next words, had he cupped palms behind his lobes like someone suffering from diminished hearing in a pantomime.

'Go on,' muttered the Italian, with supple caresses of the air, motioning for the Icelander to continue this hyperbolic narrative of historic impact. 'You saw the swans? You're having a leery grope now, aren't you? You're pulling my plonker: when and in what manifestation did you experience this impossible migration?'

Ísleifur Reykjavík sequestered himself around the pulsing red colt shying through the gloss of smoke, that burning ember between his teeth – hungry for gas, oxygen, combustible stimuli, a rotting lung, a collapsing trachea. He appeared diminished within the tweezering wingspan of a half-suffocated moth; marooned in the recent past to be confronted by majesty, and through said lens of irreconcilable humility, discover the empty value in not being able to receive or revise a miracle. Ísleifur drew wearily on his cigarette, and began demolecularising his vision: defusing particles to move beyond the building blocks of narrative – to expedite access to the overarching premise, the big picture. The friction of details obscured what was frighteningly evident: an alarming mass, clustering between his words, called Regret.

'I was with my birdwatching accomplice, Bricktop. It was a lush, froze-fresh autumn morning when the Scottish sun isn't charging over the slumbering fringes of the town but shuddering a plumage of dew-mottled daylight like some great world-scoffing roc equipped with a wingspan cut from sunset trappings over the blinking capitalist hatchlings in their workaday best beneath it: I needn't over-praise the virtues of the day, so I'll cut the crap. It was bloody stunning. A day of scandal and talon! Bricktop and I were parsing through the marshes, rationing out sticks of chewing gum and crafting our most immaculate bubbles with detonative little pops as we bustled with a jaunty tread over the wheatbelt, and I was succumbing to the sermon common to most morning-dappled ventures of companionship, presenting a philosophical discourse to Bricktop on the Socratic clarity fostered by rural splendour – all that bullshit you indulge for the sake of rationalising your socially-disturbed self-exile, out in the green dusk of the highland, when you'd rather be toasting the tips of your toes by a hearth in some cosy Edinburgh bedsit swarming with minxy bar-staff – and suddenly I tripped *right* where we're gawking with jaded brows today, and I plunged into the reservoir.

'But instead of thrashing or vomiting estuarine muck or raging against cowpats and ineffectual shoe traction, rather than churn my arms in a shocked and ornery struggle as the water weighted my clothes like chainmail, I couldn't move. I'd fallen directly into a gallery of roosting tiger swans. Red as Chinese lanterns loftily congregating the glassy canopy of the lake. They smelled like jasmine and buddleia pollen and, let's be frank, quite an abundance of birdshit. My heart recognised the gravity and divinity of the moment because it slowed down to the terminal one-four beat of a rabbit in hibernation, to reserve my energy and fear and zeal in the fat of my veins; I dared not raise my exhalations above a vigilant hiss, nor animate my limbs beyond a wader's choppied dance. The birds did not stir. I was caged between a nocturnal procession and that sun-spangled watery pit. The swans eyed me in curious repose, occasionally bridling or bluffing their feathers. Ninety-nine blood-gold luftballoons, a shivering Icelandic ornithologist, and the funky monkey.'

I was – with an unfortunate and uninitiating display of distaste – consumed by a catastrophic confusion which nimbly was superceded by a sensation that I was *entitled* to a coherent chat with this Icelandic recluse; therefore this new deviation of clarity was ungovernable.

'Excuse me,' I yammered aloud, exercising my brow muscles with a fetishistically English thrill. 'You keep referring to monkeys! I'm sorry, and I appreciate that you carry a loaded weapon, but it's becoming unnecessarily moronic, and I for one am in vigorous favour of sustaining the philosophical substance of our current discourse. So let's drop the ape jape, am I right? It's become a red-arsed distraction for me, if you'll pardon my diplomacy.'

35

Ísleifur was obviously psychologically unhinged in addition to remarkably undisciplined in his pursuit for narrative fidelity, because he crumpled his forehead in frightening tenacity and burped, 'I am, of course, intending to attribute Bricktop as the very same "funky monkey" when I divulge the expression amongst present company. I'm sorry, am I not being feverishly plain in my meaning?'

This farce of semantic miscalculation had devolved to become a savage exasperation. I said as much: 'In Christ's warped white name, what the plebeian-fuck are you hinting at, man? There can be no meaning for the term, because it belongs to the dialect bestiary of all monstrous nonsense. It's a toot of twat, sire!'

Adolfo, as satisfies his personal chameleon quest, had engineered an audacious *fade* during this debacle which still allowed him to snort in derision at my priggish and high-volume verbal misconduct without implicating any possibility at participation or collusion. He just waned his way out of our peripheries, and out of the foreground.

'I think I can decipher your irritation, Sebastian Sackworth. I may yet possess a way to afford us all a sufficient and satisfactory comprehension. I will introduce you both to Bricktop. It won't take a brutal minute.'

Ísleifur gestured for us to follow him to a lone, gnarled and provincial cypress tree violating the topographic absence of ideas perfected by his wheatfield.

I squinted my weary peepers. Through a geometric puzzle of subdued prairie sunlight I divined the hidden constant, the submerged imprint, the form composited by pixels of afternoon sky: on a branch of the cypress, about halfway down the base of the great canopied structure, was a tiny, club-mouthed gargoyle swinging distrait legs in a laconic arc from his fond foliage-castled perch. Ísleifur Reykjavík clapped his hands in uninhibited scatters of fervent cheer, swelling his cheeks into miniature balloons as though preparing to spit, rosier than a radioactive turd.

The distant figure waved back.

'There, you see! Allow me the honour to introduce you both to my companion in the threat of adversity, my singular arboreal skygazer and favourite expert in mammal vaudeville, Bricktop. *Voilà*! He's a monkey – my funky monkey.'

36

'He's a chimpanzee,' I croaked, deferring to my default status as the consummate antagonist of half-truths. 'He's a great holy black monarch of a sodding chimpanzee, Ísleifur,' I reiterated. 'Blimey fucking Iscariot.'

Adolfo craned over my shoulder with uncharacteristic restraint, his hot corrosive black-currant-buttered smirk moistening the nape of my neck. There was a fascinated horror in his lusty plea. 'Sebastian, I could've sworn we purchased business-class seats to *Scotland*, so it rapidly catalyses a fast and cruel feeling of disorientation when I see a bleeding chimpanzee lollygagging in the limbs of a larch wearing trainers and freakish white gloves.' He paused, panting, like someone who'd just fled a midnight screening of Kubrick butchery. 'Don't you agree?'

'No, I would not,' I swallowed, scavenging for warmth beneath the icy loom of this new absurdity. 'That's a cypress, Adolfo,' I explained, with fiery dismay. 'A cypress, not a larch.'

'You're quite right,' he thanked me, grave with admiration. 'Whatever must have come over me?'

I harboured no insightful response to this, but I could be certain that it began as a rattle in the circuit of the brain. A Scottish fever, toothy and wild, a tiger in the mind.

'Can we say hello?' I hazarded. 'It's only proper behaviour.'

There is a rich, bracingly nuanced, multifarious dearth of things to be said about chimpanzees, whether that assume the form of an anthropological, zoological, historical, geographical or pop-cultural treatise, but perhaps the most significant in its insurmountable delicacy of articulation is this: *these creatures are little genius fucking curmudgeons.*

I can only suggest that such a commonality of the species has remained commonly unvoiced because legitimating a sentiment underpinned by an agility and purity of perspective such as this one ("All chimpanzees are arseholes"), results in verbalising an indictment on our own humanity: the characteristics of the Great Apes remind us of our own. To motion that all chimpanzees are bastards can only accrete into one theoretical corroboration: the world is subject to the rule of tree-retreating scoundrels. This is a most distressing ontological conclusion to maintain, vituperative in its social comment, and vomitous in its aftertaste, but there can be no denying that meeting Bricktop from beneath the visored green snarl of the Icelander's cypress tree inoculated me against the sting of a scurrilous truth. *I wanted to throw my shit into Ísleifur's face.* There was a monkey in me yet.

As it was, I indulged less wanton pursuits and blew a brassy, pitch-perfect and diuretic raspberry right into the higher arches of the arboreal aberration where Bricktop now commanded reign. The chimpanzee was sweetly delighted. Hoots, vengeful smacking of the lips and a cadenza of canopied applause assailed my leering ears. My confrontational performance had yielded an ecstatic purist. He just happened to be sporting tufts of fur, an electric blue tweed jacket, white velvet gloves, bandoliers, an aeroplane necktie and was eating bananas with his feet in the mezzanine. You can't cast-audition your admirers.

'So. So this is Bricktop, the local birdwatching expert,' Adolfo wheezed, too precocious in his intellect and defiant of good sense to disregard the spectacular sloth of that tautology. He risked another scrabble for wit and yawned, 'Well, helluva fortune it must be possessing opposable thumbs when teaching a gargoyle to knot his own necktie, am I right?'

Ísleifur shrugged, as if such a calculated simulation of nonchalance exonerated him of all charges attesting to his exceptional eccentricity – for let's be brutal, the Icelander was an outstanding freak – and he cleared his throat the way a fool struggles to curry a version, a perversion, of respect. 'Do you want to see the *Cygnus toro*? Be honest with me. I know where they congregate when not at the reservoir.'

He scrutinised mine and Adolfo's startled expressions and smiled, his eyes blacker than a panther's guilt. His voice was soft and tight with smoke, and its sound lulled me into a state of mesmerised piety. 'I'm willing to direct you fellows on where to travel, if you'll offer to drive and supply me a seat.'

Adolfo was the first to crack; he blinked repeatedly like a beached catfish which has been tormented through the industrious probe of a driftwood staff. He glanced at me with the inane surprise of all those whose most deep-seeded desire will be whispered into fruition by an individual you were certain only minutes ago was preparing to blow shotgun shells through your fear-clanging scrotum. Adolfo snapped up Ísleifur's bait of unusual friendship.

'Sorry, are you promising to take us to a rookery of tiger swans? Here? Now? You know we're horrible gits, though, don't you? But listen, Ísleifur, *amico mio*, no-one has professed to a legitimate, assured sighting of a tiger swan in over *two decades*, and prior to that the creature was always discerned as the birdwatcher's cryptozoological equivalent to a sodding "phantom kangaroo". The last living specimen in captivity is claimed to have been in 1953, in fucking Mongolia! Are you seriously assaying both myself and Sebastian, here, with an unwavering promise to guide us to the feeding grounds of the legendary, even-presumed-extinct giant waterfowl, on the whimsical basis that we spilled the beans on why we're wheeling like broken dervishes out in your taro crop? Tell me you're valuing our timeless British ignorance with the snowdrop wisdom of Icelandic truth.'

I arched an eyebrow in solidarity, and made expectant pout shapes with my mouth. Within a jot – which is to say the intervening time it takes for a hummingbird to slurp a honeysuckle dry – I had lunged at Ísleifur Reykjavík for a heart-fond embrace that would intravenously transmit the fear of God into even the most wretched arbiter of sin: I can be terrifying in my display of intimacy, which might account for Pamela's allegation that I often stabbed her in the face with my knob after she suggested she'd perform oral sex on me. At any rate, I am currently in Scotland while she was probably right now entangled in a sexual fury with the British Olympic swim team for all the humour she located in the act of lovemaking, so any violences I may be faulted for in my appetites for a racy fuck can be morally forgiven in the face of my newest predicament: a broad-shouldered Icelandic birdwatcher, shouldering a rifle and squandering a grimace, suddenly overwhelmed by my crazed lunge of gratitude.

I hugged the Icelander sweetly, dismissing the stink of earwax and used teabags.

'My offer stands. If you drive me, gentlemen, I'll direct you both to see the swans,' he cringed, patting my scalp the way a child attempts a game of pingpong with their hand.

Adolfo dived into the fray, sweeping us up in a volley of friendly fire, Italian kisses consuming my complaints.

✳

Ísleifur guided the way, sweeping through the suffocating pinkening tufts of the wheatbelt just as the buttery beam of a watchtower trawls the scurrilous dark of an abandoned prison yard, and all the while he entreated – or treated – us to a rendition of a Kraftwerk dirge ("Computer World") through gritted teeth.

It might have struck me as harrowingly peculiar that we'd not yet met an authentic Scotsman the entirety of the half-day we'd squandered since assuming landfall in this green reckoning of wild landscape, but I didn't dwell on this most rampant and tangential of epiphanies, for some spectacular and fundamentally ravenous occurrences cleave a path of ruin unfit for reflection. So instead I will simply state: my mind was on the loaded shotgun still lashed tantalisingly between the Icelander's shoulder-blades, nostrils invaded by a storm of uncertain power, a sensation I now know and associate with an exclusive, prehistoric, catastrophic apprehension – *you can smell death from a mile away.*

The pox-fucked spectre with a laugh like the scattering of runes, the roll of a die, the birch-like chafe of antler locking antler, the knock on your driver's-side window by a Liverpudlian reptoid sporting more bling than functional molars, yea, that harbinger of terminally-interrupted hearts, o verily does He descend to bedevil a moment of unclouded momentum! Death regards Himself as a comedian *non pareil*, and let that be a lesson to us all. Someone whose judgement is not swayed or deviated by a stony absence of amused appreciation is one creepy fucker, indeed.

We each unlocked the doors of the brown buffalo, glowing with promise like a turd on a summer sidewalk, and fell in beside Vasquez Duchamp, who merely disrobed us all of our articles of pretension with a set of laconic sockets, so droll in their shameful emptiness that they withered our sense of adventure immediately. It's remarkable how precisely a skeleton can remind you of your growing preoccupations with dread, even if he is your ally and you angle a moth-bothered beret on his cranium at a rakish angle.

40

I set to lighting a cigarette and facilitated flavourless introductions.

'This is our dear adversary, brief companion, keeper of the flame and custodian of crocodile grins the world over: Duke Vasquez Duchamp, Esq., at your urgent service.'

Ísleifur Reykjavík refused to react, though perhaps that précis is inaccurate insofar that the statement presupposes that I could conduct a physiological survey on the characteristics of the man's taciturn squaring of the jaw, by merely observing it the way a dog-trainer ascribes value to the behaviour of a whippet prior to it keeling over from rattlesnake fever, but the result was identical nonetheless: the Icelander glanced at Vasquez as if to suggest, "I chow down a mortar-and-pestle'd sediment of human bone with my bowl of Weetabix each morning," and no fuselage of skeletal remains was going to compromise this consummation of comfort in a million years. Albeit, let's be clear, I believe the Icelander may have quelled a gulp when he noticed the ink moustache beneath the skeleton's keyhole nostrils.

None of this interfered with the macrocosmic drama unfolding simultaneously to it *outside* the protective vacuum of the buffalo, for as we sidled with gracious buttocks into the soft, yielding, absorptive gutter of obscene statesman-leather behind our car's resistant glass, Ísleifur craned around with sudden terror.

His cheeks were disarmed of their rosy, ruddied rooster-glow. He clamped teeth together and signified with a throttled sigh that we best start driving. I assumed that moment to demonstrate an alacrity of intellect and peered out through the wind-scowled glass on which my chill, sleep-hectored cheek rested – and fear in all its irrational plumage tormented me with its assault of airy beating! Something scarier than the frivolous whisper of my re-energised psychosis gnawed at me, like a Tatooine Jawa on a droid's truncated limb.

Bricktop, the chimp, had evacuated his cypress nest: the bower was free of the foreboding black grope of a jumpy, daffy, skeet-freak chimpanzee and his indigo anus. I contorted my body and shot Ísleifur's impassive, dark-pale transom of concern my own troubled glare: there was *no* pet monkey to be clapped in the chains of unbroken visual contact, no electric blue beast to whom you could jaunt your fedora at, if indeed a man can sport a hat inside a parked car and not appear arrogant or resentfully cautious about the weather.

41

Bricktop had not only tripped the light fantastic; he'd hauled it, bound and gagged, to the furthermost peripheries of the skycumference, and then launched it, within moments of grim pursuit by launching himself, over the edge of the Scottish horizon. Everything now sustained a darker, more scandalised taint. I realised we were being hunted. This whole navigation to witness the majesty of a tiger swan migration, as profane a wonder such an experience might yield, was nevertheless a contract with strings attached, and the Icelander's monkey was the puppet-master. That simian was sinister, and possessed a sordid appetite for the availability of its master the way Pamela would fuck me into submission if I wished to debate her on an emotional injustice deposed in my direction. Ísleifur was unclaimable territory. All this I assembled from the fleet second I deployed in watching the turbulent flapping of the Icelander's hands between his own knees.

'You're shaking,' I observed, narrowing my eyes. My nose suddenly felt like a momentous aggrievance to suffer; I could smell the churlish tonic of his sweat. 'Either you're melting, Icelander, or you're sluicing up a storm. What the fuck is this about?' My neck froze: not the nape, but the neck itself, like I'd been buried in a ceaseless vice of ever-tightening quicksand. I tried to swallow, but I'm certain it looked the opposite. 'Ísleifur, can you please tell us why you keep a firearm on your person *at any given time*?'

Adolfo could always be relied upon to act on the inflection or imprecations of a threat-swollen subtext (he was born in Nottingham, I remind you), and now was an occasion of scandalous resonance that resulted in no difference: he thrust the key into the ignition with such a presentiment of ease as to inspire comparisons with the speed a chain makes as it whips through a sick tree, and then his palm was gunning the buffalo into gear – an engine percolating and snarling whole moments behind his ambition.

The car vaulted from first to second, describing a sluggish toll from the embankment at the edge of the Icelander's field before belching itself into motion down the cool, violet mile of road devoid of all occupancy or motor warfare.

I swallowed my BMI in nasal junk, fingernails of my right hand monitored with tiny bites by a jaw of clenched teeth. This shit would derail a man's frame of linear wisdom. Fear is the absolute worst thing that can befall an impressionable pessimist, and the descent into uncooperative anarchy which would soon follow was a corollary of my most vestigial, seductive fascination for dread that would test my resolve. Because it was abominable, undeviatingly sacrificed of all virtue and it still disarms my wilful cheer even now – a viral memory is the most certain facility to corrupt or derange your conviction in the promise of the future. What happened next was a resulting heartbreak:

I swifted my eyes again to Ísleifur and he was squaring his jaw as if newly cognisant of the function of his nipples or the approaching barbarism, and he gripped the passenger hand-hold, bolted to the interior of the vehicle, with white-knuckle zeal: it should have populated a preposterous tableau, this moment of cinematic exaggeration, but it only released ice into my veins in frost-bustled schemes of a sly regret, deep into the channels of my blood.

I lurched to life, like my metabolism had just lunged into a speed of activity and in so doing released me from the irresolute clutch of the thaw of my fear. My mouth yawned with a start, and I blurted, "Christ Almighty, Adolfo, get us the blazers out of here, the Icelander's come unhinged!" None of which afforded my friend at the steering-wheel a chance to conduct a measured deconstruction on the logical perversions of my excited command, for within the stammer of a neutron collapse, or perhaps that of a swollen tongue, Adolfo administered his heel to the pedal in maximum efficiency and with nary a display of undermined obedience. We *squealed* to the pointy end of the buffalo's parabola, exceeding quiet philosophical claims that the car was an invention incommensurable with the purpose of stealth, and it rumbled into third before hopping into fifth at the precise moment that Bricktop lunged onto the side-view mirror, careening into the car's windscreen while scrabbling for purchase with murder in his great, glowing carnal eyes.

'*Sacré bleu!*' I wheezed.

The ape had launched itself at the buffalo, distraught that Ísleifur might forsake it to an uncompanionable exile in a wheatbelt haunted by ghosts of enduring friend-dependent discourse, a cypress tree in whose thrashing canopy past laughter and soothing murmurs from the master had come entangled. The chimpanzee had sacrificed its own intuition to continue living, its own fidelity to the value

43

of breathing, its entitlement to crave self-preservation, instead foregoing animalistic imperative for the currency commandeered by a spiritual subservience; forsaking its own life in a mission to defend the master against coercive agents harbouring malcontent lusts.

For Bricktop, this wasn't a crisis of abandonment – for there's little more exceptional a method, where efficacy's concerned, in compounding a grape-faced simian's sense of independence than shaking off his disturbingly feminine mitts, by dissolving his fellowship with the canopy: by kicking him to the kerb, gutter-side up. No: this was a retaliation to *territory*, to thwarting the treachery of a threat – a stranger – to the valence of the chimpanzee's sanctuary; not concerned with parochial notions of exile at all. Bricktop was defending the significance of sanctuary, not responding to a fear at being burdened with too much of it.

I understand this all now with the enterprise and clarity acquired through insolvent years occupied in obsessing over the intricacies, the galvanic properties of doom – usually at a bartender's expense – but in that past moment, in that car, I'm complicit in the great transgression of rejecting the painful motives of others, and in particular of that fucking sweet schizotypal beast spelunking out of the mouth of hell at our shuddering convoy: all I can identify *in the moment*, before the impact, is the inviolable grimace of towering retardation, of unmitigated and inescapable violence, of the *stunning infancy* of a berserker's psychology.

You must never forgive a lunatic his crimes and misdemeanours, because the lunatic reaps no remorse with the sickle of a fractured mind: there are some who possess the belief that because an unhinged personality devalues and desiccates the object of Reason, (and that being to vindicate the victim of said misdemeanour), by not understanding its purpose, the lunatic should be forgiven this delusion of power, the way a privileged person pities "the help". He cannot comprehend the evil he has wrought – suggests the proponent of this logic – and thus a lunatic cannot be adjudged by the same standards of ethical behaviour to which the rational man must submit.

This is unequivocal bullshit and tantamount to exculpating a psycho because his guilt is less motivated by conceptions of

44

wrongdoing: if he catalyses havoc, there's no model of impartiality that envisions the consequences of said havoc differently. In my case, when someone dies, they fucking *die*, and you're responsible regardless of how comparably your understanding of that word "responsible" is. You don't evade accountability because of moral semantics, least of all if you're a rabid, rage-blind goon of an ape. So anyway: said culprit descended upon our heads, smiling in pornographic fury.

I think I vomited in nauseated fascination, through my fingers and grit teeth.

I'd never been a substantial lover of the primate tribe, and neither had my lower intestine nor aesophagus, apparently. It fleetingly reminded me of the sensation of terminal hysteria one suffers when a man without shoes alights your train on the Epping Line after sundown.

The chimpanzee collided with the plate-glass of the buffalo's windscreen. The glass, as all convex surfaces of thin-density, torsion-resistant windowglass is liable to demonstrate, bowed with maximum elegance beneath the impact of the Icelander's flying chimpanzee, peaking into a sheer-sharp dome at the edge of breaking-point like the cornea of an irritated eye. There was no more beatific choreography than that which culminated in the explosion – the implosion – of splinters amassing, then showering over my bowed, gasping head.

The car lurched with a wild locomotion off the asphalt and over the road-studs fostering a white flank up the highway verge, squealing with a fractious speed through untended tussock, pitching me from the crumpling pinch-hold of my seatbelt and into the side compartment beneath the passenger-seat window, dispatching my tongue into the yielding roof of my palate – straight to the brain. I could taste the bloody clusterfuck of florets teeming in fungal clots off my brainstem as they succumbed to the shock of the collision. Our rented buffalo was on its last legs: it accelerated with all the thrust and none of the linearity of a vehicle in control, describing a swathing sweep of the cool grade of motorway until we were all facing sideways, the nose of the sedan directed at an oncoming frieze of fence-posts, Scottish as a stillborn Nessie and just as implacable. Fuck me did we dismally fail to anticipate the vertiginous sense of inertia which streamed out of our ears and from between our eyeteeth as the buffalo plunged glass and steel through bracken and fen. Something akin to a shuriken or a tumbling blade forged from coral inflicted a transversal cut straight to my lower lip. Blood burned from the slice. I swore, and braced myself against impact. The car cut its losses, and ploughed straight over the ditch, uprooting a line of posts, before submitting to a fever of unwholesome shakes which Adolfo responded to by applying his hoof to the brakes. The buffalo's continuing reign of baptismal fire hissed out in an instant, which sent us jolting forward, and Adolfo Cavaggio out of his driver's seat, through the glister of crack-puzzled glass, and like the fulminating glow of a cannonball of Italian design blistering the sky, was pitched over the wheel and into the night, my winged Harry Houdini howling from within a mottled coat of glass. He twinkled to death, out in the darkness.

When the members of the local constabulary for Kilmarnock had finished exchanging their disquisitions and disclosures, made the sufficient degree of performative grunting behind red tape, thrust wide their swollen Copernican stomachs, exhausted either their commitment to the banal procedures common to an underwhelming police investigation or their withstanding reserves of pen ink, had recovered the body, witnessed the pronouncement of the only available medical practitioner (a chiropodist called Fitzgibbon equipped with the alarmed eyes of his arboreal namesake, who adjudicated the affair with a philosophical "Och, he's deader than Tutankhamun's high-school sweetheart"), and had kindly requested for me to return the blanket they'd cosily caped me in to better insulate my grief, there seemed no foreseeable method to continue welcoming the rest of my days.

I drank myself into a depression from which there could be no intrusion of kindness (let's be clear, and assert that my kidney suffered no neglect or prospect from being greatly poisoned, as my thirst seemed only to concern itself with beef tea), and I woke in an amenity-scant Scottish bedsit, every few hours throughout that first week, ripe with the effluvial pall of a dysfunctional rectum, or some Chinese greengrocer specialising in packet soup. My brain hunted the shadow-goaded recesses of my skull, seeking out a quarry as morally endangered as a guilt-free memory, but every minute I found myself crushing or otherwise suppressing an arrant flicker of yearning to hear Adolfo's brassy, dumbfounded excitement percolating through the silent thaw, every minute I could not extinguish a vision of my best friend saturated in blood, his eyeballs protruding from the canopied basilica of their sockets as though peeping around a threshold to ascertain if the devil had come out to play.

Adolfo Cavaggio had been killed: that much I satisfied myself sobbing over, with long equestrian snorts of ballsy grief, as the daylight banded my inert body, sequestered on the hostel bed, before being reclaimed by the vanguard of early night, transferring the warmth in my static limbs for the cold, bitter, rapacious brand of moonbeam violence. I sat on that bed and waited, sun and stars casting aspersions about the nobility of my friendship through the reticulated blinds, as police officers burped legalese onto the bedside answering machine and snickering journalists transmogrified irony into solemn sympathy, by way of an alchemical poultice of money and professional disbelief, before assailing me with emails and handwritten envoys expressing their humanitarian craving to "set the record straight".

Just precisely *why* had a chimpanzee sporting a fine mural-patterned brocade, belonging to an Icelandic environmentalist, slung itself in front of a scrapyard turd of a rental car, to bring about the murder of an Italian wildlife photographer, on a disserviced swamp ridge, half a day's drive from the closest metropolitan habitation? Had this something to do with a legendary red swan? More importantly, was I (Sebastian Fenugreek Sackworth, English PhD candidate and antidepressant-prescribed history archivist, with a creepy fixation for researching preserved bog victims), now marooned in Kilmarnock? Did I possess the clarity of feeling to reveal my plan to the public, now that my comrade of seventeen years had been interred, violet as a Scottish loch, his flesh now stiffening around the phalanges? I *did* have a plan, didn't I? Was I scheming to hock my story, such that it was (the reporters were all politically aligned in their ardent mission to emphasise the fact that,

47

for all its exemplary weirdness, for all its defiant energy to badmouth the spurious individuality of most competing news items by its very *existence*, my story was a threadbare attempt for reality to emulate fiction, and that all it would successfully inspire was a season of similar exaggerated press, barren of substantial human interest); was it obtusely possible that I might succumb to the prostitution and packaged enticements which the highest-bidding ambassador for the glitterati might muster with their manifold desire to vindicate my interests? Could I really be *so callous* as to sell my survival, exchange my eye-witness account, remunerate my rage by accepting a price quoted to me under the table by the editorial staff of *The Scottish Telegraph* or the *Edinburgh Exchequer*? And what might that price look like? As shibboleths denoting the immediacy and lust for breaking in – for taming – a newsworthy narrative such as mine go, did it seem as though the newshounds who had already solicited me with a hard-cash offer were committed to the task of winning the rights to my experiences? Was I being pressganged into submission? If yes, *when* would I be confronting the vorpal flashbulb of the Scottish tabloid's wink? Would I be issuing a statement to the media before Wednesday? If no, was I too chickenshit to dignify my friend's passing with a lucidly-divulged, rhapsodic, unabridged, fist-pumping testimony to his untimely death, or was it merely a matter of miscalculated dividends? Come on now, you quaint London twatpocket with your Gomez Addams cowslick and your misaligned nipples (*my, these journalists were admirably well-informed*), come on, Herr S.S. Rhodes Scholar, open your pouty toothole and spill the beans: why a chimp? What a swan? How a kill? Who a fool? You a fool, Sebastian, o most agreeable truth, you a fool. Don't retreat into the reverie of heartbreak without first disclosing such an oblique, covetously golden fact: you the Poobah of Knaves, the Grand Guignol of Harlequins, *and don't you fucking forget it*.

What a bed I was now encamped on! A mattress bloating from the festive community of roaches (as green and torrential in size as tortured araucaria cones), which had long since succumbed to the atomistic half-life of groaning flesh parties, being spattered with the hints of lost ejaculations, so that even a transient proximity with this damp, rust-whorled surface beset a feeble nose with a sweat that was practically *mineral*, a musk that was *virtually breathable*. A mattress

48

that had drained scrotums, evacuated bowels, cushioned the rapist or softened the adultery. A long, pentagrammatic annexe to the deathly ideal of monogamy, this bed had weathered one thousand storms and sheltered thrice as many rainmakers. I should have felt ill, if not loathsome dwelling in the seat of such putrefaction – that crumpled summertime fuxedo stuffed with eiderdown and scuttling inhabitants – but I suddenly knew what it signified to be fully and irreconcilably and unvaryingly alone, I felt its full and pugnacious force, as I foundered in casting for sweet mercies, like the *face* Pamela would employ to regard me if I'd said something delicious or inadvertently witty, like the *embrace* Adolfo had once favoured me with, so motivated by heat and glass and coyote song and dilute summer hootch, when he was still warm and vivid enough to wrangle my squirms.

I considered my long, scrofulous fever of failings, alone in that Kilmarnock open-plan gouche, and concluded that I was a basic rube, a quintessential fuckstick, a sorcerer of entropy, a boy born to lose. I cavorted from disgust to cannibalistic self-atonement within the time it took to express my snot into the pillowcase and wail my case. Sebastian Fenugreek Sackworth: he'd finally submitted to the holistic impermanence of crippling depravity, for my girlfriend was gone, my bosom ally was slain, my country was lorded over by unsympathetic PhD supervisors, my morning's traumatic turd resembled my irreparable rental vehicle contour-for-contour, o intervene grim death! for I was otherwise only going to resort to silly irrationalities, like defenestrating my dick if the abyss continued to spiral like an imitation Twinings teabag before my horrified eyes! Help! Help! Before the cockroaches claim me.

There was a knock at the door, five times in rapid succession, perfecting a landlord's tremolo with percussive gusto. I hadn't realised I'd been screaming aloud for the past ten minutes.

The knob twisted with remarkable promise, for have you never observed that surprise moves in a clockwise direction, and a little hairy troll entered the premises while heartily imitating a policeman.

He was elated at being newly equipped with an opportunity to roadtest his vintage-model mimicry, as though an actor of the stage confiding in the confidences of the world's most exclusive audience, *vis-à-vis* this wanker ensorcelling you in this very lament, which is to say me, maestro of the fallen, Sackworth of the perpendicular nipples, because he twirled fast his baton, did this law-abiding thespian, whistling the blowziest of Trafalgar ditties like all bobby bastards, and twinkled at me through two economical, packet-pea peepers – the eyes of a stoat momentarily dazed.

'Well, this is a chummy abode, and by such qualifier I intend to denote *hospitable, charming, shire-like, picturesque, undisturbed*, owing more to the viscera of a *womb* than a *wound*, for one could mistakenly connote the signifier "chummy" and view it as an abbreviated or vernacular descriptor for "chumming", which as I'm certain you're seasoned enough to know directly refers to the act of distributing blood and less solvent carrion residue into a body of water, generally oceanic rather than estuarine, to attract the carnivorous curiosity of a shark. Which is nonetheless what you've secured in *me*, for albeit I vehemently maintain that one cannot ascribe improper or linguistically problematic signification to a word, that is to say *phonic utterance*, I must also conceivably concede that a vehicle for language, which is to indicate *you* or *myself*, are the plenipotentiaries for this administration of the spoken expression, and in so fulfilling the obligations of our social contract, must agree by our collaborative function to adhere to the grammatical and syntactical appurtenances of our socially-ascribed discourse to nonetheless call a *spade*, if it were to displace phonemes with particles of embodification and therefore manifested itself before our critical gaze, a *spade* and nothing other. And thus we arrive at our philosophical *impasse*, for though your domicile continues to pertain to the phenomena associated with its "chummy" appearance, so too must it be acknowledged that it has lured the snout of a long, rapacious, bullish bottomfeeding predator which only the transitive noun "chumming" could justify for my present preoccupation in said chummy abode. I hope you don't mind me recapitulating the aforementioned ontological *impasse* to which I explicitly refer and elaborate on its capacity for dichotomous consequence by stating: *you're fucking nicked, here, guv'nor.*'

The troll hefted his baton into his palm, and regarded me with the steeliest contour of his packet peas. Something emerged, as a thrush is wont to flush from a thicket at the height of hunting season, from beneath the bristles of his chimney-swept moustache. I was alarmed

50

to discover the fossilised bones of a smile, preserved expertly despite weathering all manner of prejudicial insult, prime among which was the response which slithered out of the soup of my palaeontological revulsion. The bobby beamed, and I baulked aloud:

'Nicked for what, you philologic clown! *You're* the one who stole all definitional meaning from the language I'd ordinarily harness for the purpose of instructing you to get the fuck out of my room! If I'm *nicked*, it's invariably of a foreseeable opportunity to inform you that there's a bridge somewhere advertising for your specialised services. I've just experienced the worst night's sleep in my haphazard existence, after bearing witness to the *murder* of my best friend, and I don't have any marrowbone for you to grind while the Brothers Grimm prepare an advertisement seeking your goat-retardant skillset, so can you please expedite your trolly carapace off my rented carpet and through my beloved accommodation doorway, from whence ye are invited to knuckle your way through the verse of fable and into the hearts of small bedridden children who will revile the shortest word of your continued exploits. And so, begone!'

The troll folded his arms, visibly affronted, and his brow darkened: somewhere an orphaned community of lightning wailed for the reappearance of its parent stormcloud. I swallowed, extinguishing the least valuable fodder of my brain down my throat and through my rectum in silent gusts of smart gas. The troll's grip on his shiny, ornery black baton tightened considerably. His knuckles pinkened, like shark pups. 'You're *nicked* because we've discovered you lied on your private testimony. You told my deputy constable that you didn't know what it was, *per se*, that had accosted your brown sedan out there, in the Kilmarnock clover. We have reason to believe we've caught the culprit.'

I wanted to react with disbelief to this claim, if not hammy moral outrage, because it's sensible to feel an obligation to defend yourself against the polemic and disparagement of those who wish to witness your fall, but my testes weren't consumed by the frivolous energy of verbal bloodlust, and my hypersensitive English heart wasn't in it enough to make a reasonable performance. I felt cold all of a sudden, like a tree newly given to an epiphany that his brothers have been vanished, to leave him desolate and standing alone on

51

a naked hill. My world had shrunk; my tastebuds had migrated to the sixth and dead cell receptor of my tongue, where papillae and all gustatory data is effaced by a cancer of blandness, the chamber of flavour where only sand, water, unshaven crotch, human hair, raw cilantro, cardboard and discount uncooked tempeh retain dominion. My ambitions had been withered and distorted by my interlude with trauma, and my shit was slithering from the faucet of my bowel like a Mongolian death worm cannibalising its own tail, so that the moment my stools were claimed by the maw of the shitter the water turned to iodine. My hopes for the future, in which I may have ascertained consolation between the tits of a Scottish dryad – her sunny orange cunt evacuating me of my mixed-up resentments for my ex-girlfriend – and the medicated cocktail I'd enlisted for my adventure to supercharge my PhD study-by-correspondence so that my thesis might arrive as a gospel envoy, an illuminated document which manifested itself uncorrupted within a meteoric night of genius, *these* hopes seemed only to have resolved the half-life of most foolish fancies.

No-one would jump my bones, I chided myself. I'd be lucky if someone even stole my skeleton. O, worthiest Vasquez Duchamp, where art thou shark-scandal'd grin? Have you, too, been reclaimed by the auditors of Hades, or the employees of the Glasgow Prestwick Airport rental car agency?

In a porous flare of recollection, I could see the body of my best friend, Adolfo Cavaggio, slain with his arms akimbo, extravagant, contorted, his legs describing tortured configurations, spastic and misaligned like a great bird, a flamingo perhaps, or a red swan, defiled by the carnage wrought by the tyrannies of gravity.

He looked truly dead in my mind. Violated beyond the ken of reckoning. An extinct species, impossible to emulate, a king among beasts, a biological peak on a latitude of underwhelming creation, a freak whose soul had cascaded light like a brazier engulfed by a fountain. I could not keep the horrors from seizing my disgustedly captivated gaze, and nor could I prevent tears from welling from my tearducts and coursing hot tracks like flame through bottlebrush down the red-buffed sockets of my cheeks. My tongue tasted the phosphor of sorrow as it betrayed my exterior, flashing in tracks down my face, and I was overcome by a flavour of whisky and bud-

52

blossom mead. I was a bird, too, I suppose, pollinating my ruination. I was a skeleton, a preserved perversion, a mummified whisper just as Vasquez had been for Adolfo and I: I would only signify a premonition of death to all those whom my brittle hand touched.

'Who do you mean?' I asked the troll. 'My friend died because he saw the demon of his future and could not repress the desire to accelerate to hit it,' I howled, trying to be cryptic enough that I didn't have to get bogged down with the details of tragedy, gaze into the fossil swamp where my friend, like all bog corpses before him, lay pickled and sporting the expression of his final strangled breath. 'Adolfo was also on drugs,' I improvised.

'Which is no excuse for the existence of a chimpanzee,' the policeman sneered, enacting the three-act vaudeville of See No Evil, Hear No Evil, Speak No Evil. 'And we should clarify that aforementioned culprit, which is to indicate the phantasmal chimp, is presently downstairs with one extremely grave Icelander, in the backpackers' bar, anticipating your reaction to a proposition that he wishes to extend to you, though, of course, you did not hear it from me, as the cuckoo put it to the jailbird. For I don't especially intend to resurrect a closed case of foreign death and reckless endangerment, because I have more sustaining ambitions to pursue, I'll make it known, including but not exclusively reduced to retiring to bed early with my fascinating reference text discussing tropical fish, of which I'm currently enamoured with the *cardinal tetra*, a specimen designed with a fetching scarlet throat whose alert, meticulous nature and swift propellant grace marks it out to resemble a bird in the water, a finch perhaps, which is not to disclose that these lofty, diversionary interests eclipse my judiciary responsibilities, nor my duty to the policing profession, for I would never abort a case fertile with criminal revelation, but it seems to me, in the way certainties converge to corroborate a man's intuition, that there's no further mystery or nuance to the narrative at hand, if you'll indulge my informal surmise. You wouldn't have to be a cryptozoological expert to recognise that something spooked the chimpanzee out there, in the Kilmarnock clover, that day. I don't think I need to explain that a shoal of fish only turns *aggressive* when they're threatened to extinction. And now your Italian friend's dead. A crying shame.'

I wiped my eyes on the pillowcase, divorcing my nasal passages of their liquid complaint. The troll shuffled like an omen on rookie assignment in the doorway, sucking the inside of his cheek, conducting a distant appraisal of my emotional collapse, littering the room with his dandruff, his intellectual arrogance, his verbal pedantry, his squalid shadow, his wharfy fetor, his fishy stink. He cleared his throat expectantly.

'What the fuck are you talking about, Boxcar Slim? What do you mean "spooked"?'

'I'm referring to the monster,' the police officer confessed with a yawn. 'Clearly.'

'The what?' I felt my sense of resolve unravel with a final flutter.

'This is a most disagreeable room. Look, your Icelandic friend downstairs can explain it to you. He's waiting with the psychotic chimp right now. Best to show some mobility. A real shame,' he repeated, with a gluttonous pause.

I blinked, for the sun was erasing my physical past, corroding away at my shadow with a white face that scattered the exterior wall of the hostel and spangled beneath the imbrication of the window-blinds. I felt dry in the mouth and chest. 'The what?' I parroted, inert.

'Eh? Oh, right. I said the "cardinal tetra". Really elegant fish,' said the troll. 'One of a kind.'

I don't frequently feel comfortable in bars, not solely because I resent the captivity promoted by a social amenity which demands that drunks and forgetters collect together to assume a fallacious presentiment of independence, of triumph over the codices of the system, but because they're inevitably populated by disturbed desperadoes haunted by thunderous indiscretions, and certainly sanctuary to an excited nest of wankers. Only in Scotland does this reflection seem to smack of philosophical charity.

The bar was packed to the rafters with all typology of unsavoury disappointment, the convocation of unenlightened and whisky-spooked pupils advancing like a recycled threat through the black watches of the night, the mouths of each sorry miscreant yawning in slackjaw defiance, each man a Persian tiger rug at this notch of the witching hour. I found myself swallowing down on stomach acid in my trauma, plunging through the conspiracy of paranoid jackdaw souls, my molars chomping away at sizeable cutlets of my sorrowful exasperation, as I clambered to the hog's teak of the bar-top, gaze worrying into the backs of bulbous, drink-softened heads.

Where the fuck was Ísleifur? Had the troll been as absent of authentic revelation, as spartan of sensible perception as a policeman whose cranial dimensions he'd inherited would generally allow? Did he really vouch with sound authority that the Icelander would resurface after seeding ruination in my life, while bringing the chimpanzee, that allegorical albatross around the neck of my deceased Italian *amicus*, into the establishment in corrosive defiance of how such a confrontation, how such a twisted heart-avenged taunt would spleen my grief, would poison my sanctuary, would impurify my spirited recovery? Did the little hairy agent of Scottish law enforcement legitimately suspect that such an arbiter of violence, such an exponent of unprovoked brutality would return to scorn the gravity of my loss? There was *no way*, no resigned trump-move chance in hell, that Ísleifur and his rattle-toothed underling from the Zimbabwean subtropics would stick around to violate the ethics and etiquette of heartbreak common to a period of mourning at the innocence of its infancy. Such a rejection of propriety would be a call to arms, a goad to war!

Such a deviation of remorse would culminate in a dispensation of human decency to a degree that might only prove to be effectively reconciled by either (a) vanquishing the Icelander and his funky monkey to the exiled spaces exclusively reserved for pariahs and fuck-ups, where the limits of civilisation seceded to the mouths of reviled sea-caves, or (b) by challenging them to a duel before conducting a furious surgery on their respective scrotums with the sharp end of a martini toothpick.

For my present state of affronted fatigue, I was perhaps unfairly favouring the latter option, if only because it would require less follow-through, but I was barely devising the most economical methods for imaginary castration when I was interrupted by the disinterested drawl of the hostel publican, who slopped a snifter of brandy in front of my sordid and gall-blinded stare, the gold

55

spillway making a glistening cuneiform of deceptive shapes before my flapping hands.

The bartender, whose face promoted comparisons with a sparkplug crafted from earwax, pointed past me into the caterwaul of the spigot-quaffing throng. He buzzed from beneath the ceiling of suspended highballs, like a modem shitting pornography, or a wasp bloodbuzzed by a draught of insecticide, and I strained my eyes in the subdued lighting to read the arcane persuasion of his chattering lips.

He seemed to be accusing the brandy snifter of something.

'Beg pardon? I'm sorry, don't mean to portray the sluggish egg, the daft coxcomb, in this intellectual breeding ground, but I don't comprehend your meaning, my salty dog of a barkeep. I don't recall ordering any swill-hold of brandy.'

'Thassa wot I ben *explicatin'*, you queer Yorkshire pudding. That fella wot's ben squattin' silent-like with his circus mistress, full a fleas, over there gone yonder corner with his mug splendid with goldilocks has squared this skull-dram of brandy with me on your behalf. He be shoutin' ye a sunny trail early on the Happy Hour chase. If I were *yon*, bless my great balls of Führer, I'd knock it back quick-pickle before he knocks you back for squiffy Thatcher-snatch lappin' ingratitude.' The publican topped her up, before restoring the bottle to its rack.

My beautiful English blue ears did not deceive me! The bartender was disarmingly adequate in his trampled eloquence. The brandy had been prepared as a goodwill gesture from Ísleifur, over in his acreage of smoky darkness, to divest me of instant resentment, at least long enough to appeal to my fondness for vice so that I might hear the bastard out. I reacted convulsively, with malevolent disgust, at this treaty of armistice, this entreaty of amnesty, this olive branch of anomie, this peace-pipe of bonhomie, but the entire turbulent wrestle with indignation really didn't sustain me, and one swig of brandy with a sublime bouquet sorted me out.

Enough linguistic bullshit, I danced with the grace and poise of Jake LaMotta in *sfumato* or a black moth around the leotard of a white flame, *enough unceasing and high-falutin' tin-fluted salutary craps shooting,* I would roll my die and give the Icelander six of the best. I slapped down the brandy glass with a swallow, was disfigured

56

in a squinting quiver by a volt of vitriolic heat straight to the porcelain synapse of my ragtime ticker, shuddered with a leer and rotated to hunt down the pretty boy from the time-scoured fjords of one week past.

There he was, Ísleifur Reykjavík, shouldered into a contemplative tangle of extremities, as spendthrift as a holiday crackerjack, as spindly as a crayfish, his blond mane of hair insulating the surrounds of his boxed-in corner the way velvet gables a coffin. He was squeezed into the pinch-hold of the bar with his face downcast into a tankard of foam, and Bricktop and Vasquez flagged him on either side in liveried waistcoats and sable-shaded corsair jackets of insensible finery, to mitigate his collapse with their own dashing sobriety.

I fell in beside them, actually opposite this triple-headed imago, and lorded over the tension of the booth by jerking forth to sally up the bowl of pork scratchings before exhorting the crunchy contents down my sclerotic throat.

I chewed and cracked and popped and seethed, like a *luchador* with a mouth full of glass. There was a wrath in me, a magnanimity that refused to be parlayed, that felt as I sat before Ísleifur and his formally-garbed litter of two with victorious patience to be altering my internal anatomy, destabilising my physiological form, monopolising my biological integrity, reconstituting the matter of my competing and fricative nuclei, hijacking my commonly-accepted environmentally-determined incarnation for its own tyrant purpose, until my heaving pant and grit teeth corroborated the behaviours of my body, now one-hundred-and-thirty pounds heavier, exploding through the musculature and superstructure of my skin, green as yellowcake past its use-by date.

My mutant self resembled the Incredible Hulk in a toupé. I was bestial in this new manifestation, transformative in my rage, and I hunched like a phosphorescent orangutan, rippled flesh irradiating isotopes of resentment, the ligatures of my muscles bursting through the dimensions of my clothes.

The Icelander was uncertain how best to react to my surly transmogrification, his eyes clustering around the lip of his tankard of stout with meek dismay like a couple of dissatisfied blowflies, and his distorted smile of prayerful resistance coerced me, in my

57

monstrous venom, to persist in gritting my teeth to hear the grief-butchered environmentalist explain his version of the Kilmarnock troll's disorienting riddle. I flashed my teeth in their predatory array to Bricktop and he cowered in primal subservience with beguilingly satisfying simian comprehension, no longer willing to risk defending the life of its master in the wake of a more formidable, authoritarian creature. With infinite wisdom, Vasquez merely grinned with Mephistophelean panic.

I absconded the tankard from Ísleifur's feeble grasp and inserted the remaining beverage, receptacle and all, into the fierce chasm of my unhinged jaw, until not a splinter of scotchglass was retained to suggest its existence save for a thumping pump-action burp which detonated through my internal synaptic highway like one sombre chord through a church organ choked with dust.

I wiped my lips with the vein-crazed plume of a distended bicep. I was electric, carnivorous. I yearned to run outside and flip cars. To knuckle-box military tanks and evade spring-propelled elephant nets. To scale high-rise towers and swat helicopters like they were sexually-promiscuous groupies. To own the streets, to plunder Scotland of its sleepy dispassion. I craved the quarantine and assault delivered to me by the military might of all mobilised Europe, the missiles engaged on my torso, forehead, spine, shoulder-blades, heart; the creeping sentience, the consumptive cognizance which derives from realising you are the enemy of the world's assembled superpowers; I raged within for the sly and providential reckoning, just a diamond-cultured chance, to confront the violence and technology of our militarised earth with two giant hulking green fists. *Wham!*

There would be indented cars, uprooted streetlights, collapsed electrical wires writhing and snapped and hissing sparks amid the power disruption, parliaments of unenslaved dogs swarming the gutters, toppled cathedral architecture, basalt stones cut with immaculate refinement now strewn along the vacant city tracts and perched like cube-shaped bricks of autumn sky in the forked limbs of Scottish maples, stained-glass treatments of the Illuminated Conception blasted into a schismatic channel of glistening sharded dust like the way cocaine looks beneath a spangle of fluorescent disco light. *Bam!* There would be displaced fence palings, shotgun shells shingling the frames of the kerb, trampled rose bushes shedding scandal-pink petals to the midtown crosswind, gusts of the stuff, police vehicles compacted into pancakes, tiny hysteric creatures in SWAT artillery and piebald-green uniform dancing around me with their mouths crowing convoluted commands into juice-box walkie-talkies, tranquilliser darts injected with elephant poisons acupuncturing my arms and the flanks of my legs, standard-issue hand grenades pooling beneath my feet like particularly disgruntled and foul-baled turds. *Kablooey!* There would be bawling children and nation-wide cowardice and mass-media tabloid fetishisation, paranoid beat cops and amped-up paratroopers and scrotums in grey-flannel suits contriving reports to the UN council and the government of Defence, electrified cats yowling in leisured panic and cocksure video-games enthusiasts shaking their fists from behind disoriented cattle and lieutenants in limousines muttering defiant orders of me through school-eisteddfod megaphones. *Pow!* Through it all, I would endure, angrier than an incendiary star, unbreakable as human story, prowling the rooftops with infinite fury, looser than an African hornet, commemorating my friend's death with a vigilant vengeance that no weapon of human fancy might suppress.

I could just as easily dispossess Ísleifur of his head with a vicious jerk-and-swivel, impale it onto a bayonet and parade it through the sleeping streets, but I needed to hear his reconfiguration of the troll's bristle-faced *longueurs* if I was to get out of this fucking country of horrors, red swans and substandard butter crumpets. So I sat, green with ire, my heavy breath ventilating through me like a thoroughbred's pant, waiting for the Icelander to desist in spacing out, in a morose zen, over the suddy cream of cinnamon stouts past. It took about five minutes, by which time Bricktop and I had begun mucking about with a few games of brow-quarrelled *janken*, my Rock trouncing his Scissors like a solitaire triumph.

'You seem cranky tonight, Sebastian Sackworth,' he croaked, his chin wobbling around the cradle of his cupped palm, elbow at an acute angle that contradicted his beer-supple, misery-softened slump, a smile like a question uncertain of its own impact dictating his face. 'Would you care for another brandy?'

'I should ask whether you'd welcome another tankard,' I deflected, resisting any attempt of the Icelander's to avoid apologising directly

59

for the brazen nature of his reappearance, the psychological imbalance of his chimp's neural chemistry, the unforeseeable demise of Adolfo, the irreconcilable haemorrhaging of my thrill to continue living, the loathsome manner in which the true geometry of the Icelander's secrets had only been gleaned through the prism of distanced inquiry, the fact that my flight into Scottish self-exile had left me charting my fingertips through a future of blood in a misguided gamble of clairvoyance, striving with ghastly folly to pry open my best friend's eyes as he burped his last breath in a geyser of body fluid, a font of dying rain, beneath the headlamps of a brown buffalo, while looking for some barbarous, unnecessary and fabled fucking bird.

Most of all, I blamed the Icelander for the society and emotional remoteness and irrelevance of birds, that feathered people who seemed to reign over us all with economy of presence and with illicit incentive, perhaps waiting for the epoch in which humanity jettisoned our limbs to reunite with the worms so that their beaks might claim the kingdom which had eluded the diffuse protests of thrashing wings for so long. Oh yes, the birds could go get fucked best of all! Did I care now for a swan? For Pamela's lost hands, her encouraging caresses, her soulful breath, her detonative body, her friendly counsel, her sex-teased hair, her sheet-disrobed vestige of the bed, her immaculate patience, her unstoried sense of lacerating irony, her naked shoulders, her crying eyes, her horrified gasp, her bloodless and desperate countenance, her struggle to understand that I'd cheated, *I'd* been disloyal to *her*, I who had been privileged with something so authentic. Did I miss that bird? That morning melody? That squabbling beauty? That adored thresh of wings? That moment of rupture, when a flock aloft dissolved into an isolated navigator once more, that moment where my partner was ejected from my air-bonded stewardship to seek other flocks, elsewhere, because I'd been a bigamist, a cuckoo, a vulture in waiting, did I miss that fall? Did I ache for thermals on which I coasted to twin with her own trajectory once more? Did I need anything other than the dead in the ground, anything other than victims petrified by change, anything of the forgotten sky any longer? I resolved to feel beneath responding to these conundrums – grounded beyond migrating storm-flung philosophies – if only because it would permit me to believe I was not an injured arsehole, lost now that my promise of assuming great heights had been crippled. Did I need a swan to justify this pain? Did I want to repair a damaged nest? Was I willing to kill myself? Did Pamela keep me awake with sorrow? But how can you convince anyone to love you, least of all yourself? No: I did not need to believe in fables. If they were of any value, the fables would need to believe in *me*.

I squinted out the door as the bell chimed to admit entrance to another idiot seeking insulation against the world. Behind him sounded the eerie song of starlings through the clustering streets. Their plumage looked English in my mind's-eye, red and blue, a warfare of union jacks, braced against the toll of the wind: not a sentimental vision, for the birds looked tired behind my eyelids, but a daft one because the birds looked at home in this ridiculous country. They congregated.

'I want to stay in Scotland,' I announced, to my profound surprise. 'So tell me what you know, Ísleifur.'

He blinked at me with sudden clarity, as if I'd delivered him from a land consumed by fog into a well-lit morning arcade.

'I'll do my best. There was a beast,' he replied, swallowing. 'That is to say, some believe there is a beast. It may have been responsible for Bricktop's outburst. His momentary caginess, his raging dance. Jesus, you must understand: though this sounds remarkably metaphysical, there are always external factors of influence.'

'My name is Sebastian,' I parried, perfectly hating myself for it. I breathed in through my nose, and it felt as though the merest plume of oxygen was having to circumlocute a great alien mass within my nasal cavity, something belligerent towards the subtleties of taxonomy, like an ulterior lobe of my cerebellum, or a brain polyp which had dropped a line into my nasal canal to feed on snot and had since taken up residence by implanting itself into the septum walls. Junk rumbled within my nostrils like bones, migrant vertebrae. Maybe I housed an intruder, like Martin Short in *Innerspace*. Perhaps microscopic people had been inhabiting the aqueducts of my brain for years. Synthesising microcosmic cities within the arteries of my grey matter long before I might formulate an original, uninfluenced thought. It had probably occurred when I inserted that pea into my nostril for dinner entertainment as a mucky-cheeked six-year-old

61

braggart. Had I ever squeezed it out with a fast breath? Had it been a tiny vegetable craft? They did refer to an armada of peas as a *pod*, didn't they? I suppose I should've been alarmed at how paranoid I was becoming over a runny nose, but my reaction and subsequent tangent of reflection were vital safeguards against me erupting into a violence as Ísleifur spoke.

'You sound sniffly,' he ventured. 'Do you want a tissue?'

'Look,' I reproached, tenting my hands to exercise what is referred to during hostile corporate takeovers as a Teepee of Power. 'What are you talking about, you wilderness-crusading freak? Is this some inchoate riff on the Hounds of the Baskervilles, or is there a genuine lick of evidence that might rationalise all these hydroponic herbal suggestions?'

'Would you like me to answer that frankly, Sebastian, or would you first prefer a moment to swab your snout with some two-ply paper? I've got some tissues that are pineapple-scented. Or would you rather the aloe vera?'

'Just answer the fucking question!' I roared, thrusting my fist into my outstretched palm at the precise moment I sneezed a stockpile of chunky mucous onto the Icelander's ludicrous face.

He sagged, retreating into his cloud of defeatism once more, like a mime who'd just been remanded of his busking license. He sat between the mournful brown ape and the amused surgeon's skeleton and mopped his face with an industrious survey of his sleeve.

'I'll have the pineapple-scented,' I clarified, queasied with surplus humble pie. I blew my nose into the outstretched flourish of two-ply tissue. It really did remind me of Jamaica. 'Sorry. I didn't mean to exceed critical mass like that. I'm a little beleaguered at present, a little adrift. I just had a Scottish policeman trespass into my hostel room to accost me with a diatribe concerning monsters in Kilmarnock pastures. You mentioned beasts, so explain to me what is apparently patently transparent to everyone but me.' I transferred the used tissue, a wet tropical package of nasal architecture, into Bricktop's extended paw. He tucked it away with fastidious kindness, inside the recesses of his funeral shirt, with nary a smack of his lips. 'Better yet, Ísleifur, I want you to take me to it.'

Ísleifur regarded me with chronic, somnambulist, haggard eyes. They mustered about his sockets with lazy intelligence. He propelled himself off the cold tavern wall and regained his hunched yet unabsented posture. His fingers busied themselves with a few modestly audacious charlatan tricks, including extracting the vial of salt from Vasquez Duchamp's accommodating earhole, whilst he contented himself with complex thought.

'I can do that,' he exclaimed, once the silence had developed its own aesthetic tedium. 'What we're discussing, here, is a creature that few people have ever confidently seen, let alone scientifically or dependably identified. There is a modern lore of Kilmarnock – a local mythology you might say – which fixates on the notion that a beast dwells out in the Scottish highlands to induce a pathological fear in all manner of wildlife whom come into contact with the menacing animal. I won't dispense with all critical, theoretically-keen, rational contemplation and confess to having *seen* the thing – for I am no self-educated, rural-supped superstitious local – and I generally pride myself on administering the mechanism of sceptical analysis to something as fantastical as pseudoscientific allegations of monster inhabitants, or eye-witness accounts that suffer from generous fireside embellishment. But I *can* assert, and will continue to maintain, that something, some invariable interloper occupies the mountain pastures of Kilmarnock. Forget your blasted scarlet swans, if you want to bear witness to an unquantified species of Scottish fashioning, of rumoured majesty, it's pertinent to this discussion that you appreciate the *trust* I'm investing in you when I uninhibitedly vouch that though I've yet to *see* the creature, I've discovered evidence attesting to its existence up and down the peaty coast of East Ayrshire, from savaged and dying lamb calves, to mutilated cattle, to wide-eyed backhoe-wranglers and gobsmacked orchard farmers who bitterly admonish all unwarranted criticism to persevere in claiming that they witnessed the movements and behaviours of the monster in their apple groves. And I've heard the *screams.*

'You may construe that this foray into hysteric sobriety, into zealous seriousness, is just a rampant rant that belongs to some other version of events entirely, some other narrative of excess and distorted logic, but what I'm vehement about is only that you pay attention, that you accept the significance of what I'm confiding: there is a creature terrorising the countryside, and though you may react

63

to this banal deviation from the locomotions of sensible experience, and refuse it on the basis of cliché or lack of verisimilitude or rhetorical theatrics, I'm compelled to defuse your armoury of irony, to surpass your mocking disbelief, by offering you the following. Why is it, do you wonder, that I keep a loaded shotgun on my person at all times? I've heard the sodding screams, Sebastian, the wails that disrupt a rooster's sleep from fifty kilometres away, the castrating yelps emerging from the mouths of innocent women who have been threatened, young farmhands and withered roustabouts who caught a freakish glimpse of the beast within the high-traction beam of their braziers and headlights, and I can impress on you the fact that the *reason* you can't ever capture a photograph of your blessed *Cygnus toro* is because something is actively threatening the migration!

'There is a devastating animal, Sebastian, much fiercer than a territorial bald-arsed ape. If I knew what Bricktop knew, I would be courting wisdom to fang myself in front of the nearest passing car as certainty of escape, a pace-setting risk for sanctuary, but I know this provokes you to hate me to say it.'

Ísleifur studied my eyes, dogged me with his own until I felt as though the quiet and worst tear, the unquenched and most vindictive tear, sorrow so thorough in me that it crazed at me within my gallons of speeding blood, would surely vacate me: leave me aching for a friend whom it had been my duty to safeguard.

'But I'd admire your silence, Sebastian. I gawk, in strange affection, at the way you preserve your resolve. And what the fuck do I know? I'm an Icelandic spook, after all. Fancy myself a famed eccentric naturalist, like Darwin, or Diane Fossey, or Siegfried and Roy. Frankly, I'm a little fucking insane.' He smiled, relaxing around the teeth, bracing me with his unpasteurised milk-blue eyes so that I laughed at the lunatic slouched before me, the head of a Nordic Jesus, the body of a starved silkworm, the sort of botched beauty to once have jammed with The Beach Boys before artistic differences conspired to judge it as unfulfilled, inadequate, and so doom it with those qualities.

He reached across beneath the tabletop and squeezed my knee. 'So I want you to find it within your appetites to forgive my rampant disorder of mind and odour – because let's face it, I stink like brain-meat on the peak of a fly's wings. Anyhow, here's my proposition. To make amends. To win your trust. I have a friend for whom you may be able to work. If he employs you, you will inherit a reputable and splendid weekly income, and receive permanent accommodation to pursue your bog studies. It would also give you the opportunity to observe both the *Cygnus toro* and the monster in their undisturbed element, and if you took enough pictures of either, certainly of both, you could make your fortune and absolve any doubts as to your Italian friend's genius back home in the printed rags of Mother England.'

A spasm of resentment shot through me, disgruntling my venal pout, but I waited an empire for the gall to pass and when I felt of a mind to entertain notions of charity, such as working for a worrisome friend of the Icelander's, I invited Ísleifur to bewitch me with the particulars of his proposal.

'What's his name? This aberration of humanity? And how can you be so sure that he won't wish a terminal evil on me after I agree to work for him? I'm not exactly canonised for my illustrious history of employability, I'll have you know. I'm a keen mind with research and the labours of detailed documentation, but when it relates to interacting with the public, I fear I'm as useful as a phosphorescent ear.'

The Icelander locked his eyes with my own, and I felt a blast of Nordic chill arrest the protestations of my raging brain. He folded his hands and I felt something between Neuro-Linguistically Programmed and cross-cultural brotherhood.

'The man's name is Padraig Dunlap. He lives out on the coast, near the River Irvine, on the East Ayrshire lowlands. That's all you have to know. The rest I can arrange. Listen, what you do out there is ultimately governed by your own eager English whim. No-one else needs to know. Just understand that the man you meet out there is the closest arbiter of wisdom on this monster you seek. Defy or dismiss Padraig Dunlap, and you forego the chance to compete with hell.'

'What makes you think I want to do that? I'm a sensitive, bookish type.'

'I know,' Ísleifur Reykjavík purred, offering me the aslant glance of a blue lynx. 'That's why you get to take the funky monkey here

65

as protection with my frankest blessing. Now, give me your phone number. I may yet need to communicate with the man who avenged his friend's death to unforeseen acclaim. For I can see a future of victory in you yet, Sebastian Sackworth of the Hulk-like ire. Even with your perpendicular nipples. Mark my words.'

✡ ✡ ✡

Koun (n.); _Tuiteamas_ (n.) – A Memory; An Interruption

Pamela was never one for volubly expressing her sentiments of resentment, or for even displaying the person for whom she maintained said romantic disdain the adequate generosity of allegiance to simulate the impression that you *were in the shit*, so it always constituted a project of erroneous guesswork to conclude when she might next flay you for your unconvincing indiscretions.

The point was that she was not always *fair* in the manner of her conduct when she assembled to confront you with evidence attesting to your "bohemian immorality", because she was less likely to feel the infliction of pain from behind her armour of judgement. She would salvage her injured strength to disarm you of your phantom pride. I won't pretend to claim that her tyranny of loveless disavowal was the primary motive for my disloyalty, because if I was honest I would suffer ownership of some pretty fucked-up vices, but I won't promote the thesis that suggests love is secure under scrutiny, either. There's a triumph to a partner's watchful examining, an inequality of trust, a violence of fidelity, that even I am disposed to correlate with "cheating": if your ambitions for love are contrary to your own partner's, then how can you expect to foster sympathy, convey compassion, contribute to a coherence of desire?

Anyway, I can't demand forgiveness for my transgression, especially not from the person whose heart I had omnificently spurned, and unvaryingly not in the context of my reckless sex with a torpedo-breasted ebony lass whose name and hue was *Honey*, for I exercised thrusts with my pheromone-bloated wang at least sixty times in a space of fifteen minutes (we were both on dirty cocaine, and laughing so that the sonic ripples transferred between our flesh like salmon cross-stream), and not once did I dispute my appetite to coerce this tenthook-nippled lush with her speckle-lepered eyes into thunderous pleasure, though I had long disreputable seconds during the shagging, when no distraction except Honey's purring could have distorted my comprehension of the sin, so to negotiate or pitch at being bequeathed *anyone*'s moral solidarity would be an athletic feat not even my swollen cock could reconcile.

I neither warranted justification nor clemency, for I enjoyed myself too much, but Pamela's antagonism in the winter of our romance exacted a damaging impact all the same. The fact is I still dearly craved her – loved her, even – but she did not admire me the way she once had when we'd met at a seminar on Palaeontological Anthropology and had exchanged numbers/cocktails/cab-fares/genital juices the following week. Pamela had forgotten to be surprised by my opinions. She'd relinquished the duty to find me fascinating, to seek still to study, to debate, engage me viscerally on my *feelings* about the affairs of our veering, breakneck planet: I was no longer attractive for my human qualities: to her, I'd become a dick by convenience.

So I'd reacted by reclaiming the sole item of mine still germane to her, and I'd offered it with a savage retaliation to someone else. I wanted to discern if Pamela could love me still if I'd thwarted her access to that paltry singular convenience, if she could locate redemption in my many neglected capacities.

Of course, at the very instance of acknowledgement, when she would see me again for something other than a welcome fuck, at that ontological awakening, said acknowledgement would become corrupted, because she would simultaneously have to grapple with the realisation I'd granted someone else that welcome fuck and so hate me for the same qualities that I'd been striving to convince her to love again.

To cheat is to gamble is to sacrifice is to lose: what you *gain* is the deliverance yielded by punishment, but what you *forego* is the victim whom you hoped would only care enough in the first place to disqualify the cheating.

Such a shambles is human desire! You undermine your advantage at possessing, of obtaining that which you seethingly seek because it's all too tiresome, too complacent, too unlustred, too suck-arse to dwell in a seat of satisfaction. Stability doesn't excite, it sedates ambition. Or so you convince yourself when you're young, with

67

heaving sap-fattened testicles, stalking the elite haunts of rain-battled London, exchanging sneers with bodyguards who hulk behind red wharf-rope presided over with a little metal hook, custodians whose sole skillset is empirically qualified by how successfully they can operate the sickle-shaped clasp to grant admission to schmucks, tramps, miscreants, ball-breakers, pug-faced goons, American expats with audacious shoulderpads and fearfully tiny wallies, wallets with greenback suits and pennywhistle credibility, hatchet-men, disco junkies, shift-workers, raincoat ghosts, fuckups and burnouts and post-graduate philosophy scholars and transsexual volleyball enthusiasts, speed-grifters and monkey bellhops and pimps with chronic fatigue and failed novelists with ineradicable bar tabs.

Behind them all skulk the leggy chanteuses in their cheetah-print thigh-highs, their wry toothy mouths, their pendulous tits, their scandalous stink of woman, of legitimacy, of moral certainty, the tarty taste, the sexy skates, the tattooed décolletage, the cunning tongue, the iron fist, the velvet glove, the one you missed, the crucial chance for love.

None compare with Pamela. None defeat her grace. But she fell out of love with me long before I with her, and I could have slid inside any number of Honeys, as pelvic and hugging and distressingly adored and scorch-skirted as they may be, thumped their wet snatches and jetted in their hair every night 'til the combustion of the sun and I would still be barren of Pamela's engulfing grace. I would still groan to a loathsome wakening the following day, leaking bourbon and sweat and fever ills the next morning, with the wrong woman asleep beside me, another opportunity to win back the girl I threw away, another staked claim chalked onto perspiring flesh, a headache the size of a Mekong catfish turd wrestling behind my eyes, and my unwashed attire smacking of fart, of sea-otter, of mutton piss, of oyster jelly.

I am not a heroic man. I am not a sentimentalist. I am not a dependable catch. So I accept that Pam reacted to my romp with Honey with a final conviction. Regret for a lost beauty scorns you by its permanence: I was in the apartment kitchen when it happened, and Pamela was looking as marvellous as ever.

A wreath of powdered suds and soap-churn festooned my fingers, the previous day's dishes storied with the narrative waste of yesterday's dinners, and the entire concave dip of the sink-basin teeming with bacteria, food detritus, scales of flesh chafed off my fingertips and the most guilt-soaked human reflection likely to shimmer amid foam and disinfectant. Fuck I looked ghastly, like a chorizo sausage with leprosy.

There's something about the tedium of domestic obligations which reinforces the significance of romantic betrayal, as though the terminal mediocrity of the household chore engages with a symbolism which would otherwise remain dormant: you've not only been *disloyal*, you're pretending that scouring a few plates will equip you with the precedence for goodwill that promotes you to feel you can call it *Even Stevens*. How familiar it must feel to be arm-deep in a trough of scum.

And I was just toiling to disturb and usurp the remains of a Korean *Kimchi* pancake which had failed to assume any viable or appetising form, so that it had transfixed itself to the blade of our flute-edged spatula, *an affliction in boiling water*, when I heard the phone ring.

The crusted mollusc-like folds collapsed through my fingers in a slurried rinse of cabbage foulness, and Pamela picked up the receiver. My guilt-harassed hopes for a conjugal amnesty from Pam were for nought but my own delusionally upbeat folly, and I recognised this with a jungleburst of sun-baffled clarity the moment my girlfriend of three years swallowed after she'd asked for the caller to repeat themselves. Yonder stretches my exile.

I swifted on my heels to intercept her reaction; to read her expression. Pamela was clutching the receiver to her left ear, but though her grip seemed chokelike and empurpled the arm with which she engulfed the phone was somehow simultaneously rattling in a display of windswept strength. My nerves were shot, her mastery of tolerance was jangled. Her hands were shaking like the camera-lens of an illegal pornographer in blue-collar country. I needed to intervene before ruination claimed my name.

'Pamela,' I instructed with a decisiveness in my voice which I felt immediately betrayed my artificial demeanour, strength roaring through my bloodstream like wind through a lion's mane, 'Put down the phone. Whatever she's fucking saying, it all amounts to a dark, dislocated shrike-wincing screed of bullshit fantasy. Look at me,

69

Pam,' I stormed, casting a canopied shadow all through the narrow swerve of the apartment. 'Hang up the fucking phone. She's a crazy drug-addicted shrew, and whatever she's telling you, whatever etherised dissection of my character she's performing, whatever heinous, barbarous, uncivil and bullshit claims she's alleging, don't give a moment's credence to her. Hang up the phone, Pam.'

I was toppling now, my authoritarian reserve was exhausted, I was as diminished now of retributive conviction as a meat-contented maggot, sluggish as a shark sundered of its fins. This was my position, this was the limit to which my internal competition had delivered me, this was the culmination of my corrupted ambitions which resulted in my most spectacular failure. 'For Chrissakes, Pam, you've gotta believe me, I did not shag the girl! It's a lie!'

Pamela watched me trembling for a flame-absorbed minute, with a hand cupped over the receiver, before whispering into the mouthpiece, eyes still locked with mine, 'Sorry, I just had to check with my partner. No, we don't need a new broadband network server, we're quite happy with our current service.'

She hung up, with monstrous calm, and pointed from me to the door. This all happened within a duration of two to three minutes, and it's a superb reflection on the irresolute, ungraspable nature of tragedy that it seems to disrupt a life and leave a passage of havoc and fracture within the time it takes to evacuate your bladder of freeflowing piss. I watched her judge me, implored her to reconsider, glimpsed a new future barren of confusion: I would be miserable.

'I thought it was someone else,' I croaked, dizzy with stupidity.

Pam nodded, once, and folded her arms. 'So did I, Sebastian.' She gestured to the door, eyes brimming with hot regret. 'Collect your stuff and get the fuck out. I won't repeat myself.'

I knew I'd lost, and felt irrational, hastened, compelled to defend my cowardice, retain her admiration, lure her into submitting to one final fuck but none of it would accomplish an eclipse of what had been declared to me through Pamela's own bared teeth. So instead I hung my head, and sighed, stood sequestered in a prison of my own devising; divided from the one I loved by the damage I'd strewn.

'She meant nothing, Pamela. It was an orgasm, not an affair of the heart. I was petty, incredibly foolish, unfair and selfish and scrofulous and hurtful. I'm sorry. I'm so frequently dispossessed

70

of good sense, because I haven't figured out how to contain my impulses, not in any discerning systemic manner so that I might avoid injuring the ones I love. I'm irresponsible with privilege, and I deserve blame.'

'Sebastian, don't morally exculpate yourself in the future because you've admitted to your grievous failings. That would be one sure way to pretend you didn't just break my heart. Now get the fuck out.' She rotated to present me with an image of her back.

I did what she demanded, slinking close to the cool of the cement, made a shabby departure, thinking two words the entire time I stood beneath the apartment alcove, sighing smoke through a treatment of misted rain.

'Beautiful bitch,' I muttered, dry-weeping with bloody remorse.

A taxi came by later to unburden the street of three years of junk disinvested of its use or sense because it represented only half a collection. I squelched wetly into the passenger seat, and lamented the excesses of a weekly cab-fare.

'Where to, buddy?'

'Hm? There's a lively chauffeur. Take the scenic route downtown.'

A day later, after cutting my losses at the hostel and decamping into an outer-city bus with Bricktop's hot, upholstered palm clasped in my own – the chimpanzee remaining stridently foregone to the idea he now belonged to an English tourist with post-traumatic distress and a couple of hundred bog bodies shy of an academic tenure – and Vasquez Duchamp dismantled in a jigsaw fashion of porcelain portents in my overhead luggage, dizzied before a surf of green highlands and violet heath, the bird with the raygun tattooed to her inner wrist stepped wrathfully into the empty aisle.

She ditched herself, with a brisk sulk, right beside Bricktop as he brooded with a mystified interest over a bushel of apples in a nylon-net bag which I'd conveniently disrobed into his lap, and she slumped with mendacious melancholy into a paperback of *V* by Pynchon. I swallowed and braved a stealthy glance, studying her mohawk (which was pink with *Tank Girl* toxicity) and her arcane jewellery (she sported something quite remarkably similar

71

to a fishhook in her lower lip), before I discovered with a protean discomfort that I was transfixed by her smile, actually a kind of cruel sneer disfigured by beauty, and the shape of her neck (tapered and haunched with a network of invisible muscles, like an eland's). There was nothing vaguely unique about her (I'll be the first to void my plight for indivisible love and confide that my ardour extends to most stern, horny pale girls with abusive fathers or turbulent lusts for geek pursuits, like roller-derby or vampire porn), but Betty-Blue Raygun, with her gaze like twin indigo coves, certainly summated everything I expect is unadventurously transparent about me:

Sebastian Fenugreek Sackworth covets an unhealthy *tristesse* for women who will only unabashedly fuck him up, a concupiscent yen for lady wraiths who look excellent in fishnets and stilettos as she's leaking black Maxx Factor tears down a face svelte with fashionable starvation while explaining why you're boring and probably gay. I'm forever succumbing to the incapacitating idea of a "sexy female", but cannot locate any extralinguistic solace in this, some physical avatar for stable romance, beyond the illusion that an object of desire is capable of being mastered when it's beyond the width of human reach. I drive myself berserk to possess a seduction which began in my own head. I know this; and yet when I'm confronted with a firecracker of femininity, snarling and thorny and throat-wateringly transformative and candid with curves, I find myself retreating to a regressive state in which my brain prolapses from my body and my sperm count swells to tidal-migration numbers. It is a perfectly-observed chemical imbalance: the scent of a woman, or a certain demographic, will catalyse a bloodrush to one physical locality on my body. But empirical science can never convincingly interpret the next phase of my condition, which is to dispense with all logical interference consuming my cerebellum and agree to allow my dick to operate my mouth, just once, to yelp, "You have brilliant eyes." What immediately follows is the thunder of English manners as my sperm recede and synapses russet forth to qualify the few ways in which what I've just confessed is true and has nothing to do with sex.

'Ahem. They remind me of John Coltrane. Not the man, specifically, but his music. *Blue Waltz*. Lame, I understand, but also quite factual.'

72

Betty-Blue Raygun folded the ear of her page, and smouldered at me from between two glorious tits and one tempestuously rotten smile, refusing to correct her slump.

'Oi, Jeeves, you pulling my plonker? They're ugly eyes, and they won't be charmed or softened by your pretty and baffling metaphors. Tell you what, you can fuck off, Charlie. I don't like Sassenach twats.'

I demurred with a mournful grin. 'Absolutely, my fondest apologies to you, my bonny lass. You much prefer your dreamy Yank hyperbole, of course.'

She appeared to simultaneously loathe and savour my sceptical rebuff, and thus attacked me with a zealous splendour: 'There's nothing the least bit unnecessary or lacklustre or convoluted with arid pretension about fucking Pynchon! I'd much prefer wrangling with difficult American literature, supercharged with imagination and belly-fire, than some prancing wank-foiled coquetry of British parlour fiction, ripe with sweet-tea halitosis and besmirched by tiny wagging Edwardian dicks. The fuck do we need another armchair luminary expounding on the parlous freaking canon of Kingsley Amis. The world is scandalised with bitter, conservative, limpid and economical verse. It's an aesthetic and political gambit to epistemologically *refuse* the counsel of commodity-sensitive commercial publishers and generate a work of artistic rigour and discursive prose which yearns to be acknowledged for its commitment to problematise the prohibitive guidelines of intellectual traditionalists. That an individual might tower above the architecture of bucolic mediocrity and risk envisioning the depths of the world rather than the conventions of a uniform type of house, of an outmoded microcosm, that warrants *worship* – that betrays a sense of adventure so few practitioners are willing to admit to harbouring! Of course I delight in "dreamy Yank hyperbole" as you disdainfully ascribe it. Better that than a limp Sassenach masculine offcut.'

I couldn't delude myself that this frightful raving hussy, so poorly contained with a confluence of cynicism and ire for the hypocritical operations of society, wasn't precisely the sort of venomous harlot I thrilled to experience seesawing energetically up and down onto my balls, but her aspersions against my nation's historical tendency to favour impotent art inflicted a fierce cut in my pride and I resorted

73

to baiting her to avenge my wounded and repugnant sense of futility. I twisted in my seat as the bus lumbered through a series of potholes deep with water like an ecosystem of circular ponds, detonating our surrounds with lashings of soil clods and rainwater. We sheltered behind glass as our convoy was repeatedly pelted, casualties in municipal warfare.

I raised a disapproving eyebrow at Betty-Blue Raygun. 'I resent your persecuting allegations that all English men are, to borrow your boorish slur, "limp" or in possession of negligent shrunken genitalia. I'll have you know that such a raucous claim represents a gross undersight on my, aha, part.'

Betty-Blue's face relaxed at the very moment I'd assented my frustrations, as though she could now unavoidably discern just what febrile, basic, indecent and bestial motivations were influencing my opposition, and she suddenly must have felt flattered, even titillated, because her scowl collapsed with an inward grace to reveal a disarmingly flirtatious grin, one in which her teeth emerged to admire me.

She was on much surer ground with the banal vexations of an erotically-staggered goombah with panting eyes and an improvised tent newly erected at the crotch of his pants. She was suddenly extremely attentive, eating me up with an invasively desperate stare that recalled the way the tines of a dessert fork denuded a slice of sponge cake – vicious and rhythmic like an assault by Lou Reed's flower. She laughed then, displaying a flash of gums, and she extended a hand over Bricktop's downturned dome which I intercepted, shaking her fingers while being privileged to the percussive clatter of her many vine-wrought wristlets as they clashed down the length of Betty-Blue's arm.

We would be destined to fuck, of course, if I wasn't expected to chaperone a brown ape and a skeleton companion in secret disarray, while travelling an hour by bus specifically for the purpose of hunting an enigmatic job offer. As it was, I was resolved to accept another sweet possibility being dissevered of its nucleus of actuality if the girl didn't then defy the conventions of propriety and point with a mesmeric calm to Bricktop's silent, cogitative slump of lumpen muscle and negotiate the inward-facing design of the seat so that she was now folded onto her knees. She jostled the chimp at the elbow, but (perhaps because of the display of incandescent closure with which Betty-Blue commanded her immediate environment, including that of the homesick simian) she catalysed no disgruntlement or rancour from Bricktop, and in fact appeared to soothe rather than madden or provoke the smiling primate.

'Oi, sailor. How's about I show your little furry friend here a good time?' she percolated, humming with a kindness that certain animal rights advocates would be pressed not to construe as unsavoury if not illegal. 'I've got *just* the thing for a creature of hotblooded appetites and primal instincts, now, don't I?'

This rhetorical conundrum troubled me with amazing pulchritude, a moral threat to my orthodox gleaning of what a voluptuous agent of feminine mystery should and shouldn't do with a tree-scrabbling epigone of the hunky monkey tribe. Primary among my latitude of acceptance was situated a disapproval of bestiality, even of the softcore naked woman-astride-a-horse variety. There was nothing especially ambiguous or indiscreet about such feelings: ideological relativity didn't enter into the equation, because a desirable human female was as sexually asynchronous, as diametrically opposite an adolescent male chimpanzee as an erotic commodity could get, and no example of post-structuralist postulating might explain how a woman fucking a lemur was ethically sound.

I lurched forward to intervene in whatever Betty-Blue's debaucherous scheme may yield, investing my reach with the purest liquid muscle I could summon, but she'd already taken Bricktop by the hand at this point, intertwined digits with his like a transmammalian vice and lead him into the aisle of the bus with deranged stealth of limb.

Was this murderous Scottish bird going to have her way with my newfound animal familiar, right in the thoroughfare of our Killie town Stagecoach? How many times? I was obligated to stop her. The emotional trauma she would inflict on such a patentedly-conflicted brown ape the likes of Bricktop would be ominously incontrovertible. The minx might argue that she was being tender, even eleemosynary, but the eel was only simulating horripilation, frightful shocks that were the artefacts of a psycho brain. Surely she wouldn't sink so low, seduce my chimp and go at him solo? I would fly-kick the creep, as

75

favourable to mine eyes she remained, direct to her throat. I would find myself surprised that this all lead me to a moat.

'What the hell are you doing?' I shrieked, but covertly enough not to disconcert or alert our ruddy-eyed sweetheart bus driver.

Betty-Blue proceeded to lead Bricktop to a vacant seat at the rear of the bus, and in extraordinary fine taste produced a Rubik's Cube from her person, having extracted the plaything – that cheerful schizophrenic obelisk – from her saddlebag before thrusting the diversion into Bricktop's animated mitts. The ape was overwhelmed with the thrill of the puzzle. He squatted soundlessly onto the unoccupied seat and, with nary a wink at the potential for Betty-Blue's perfidy, immersed himself in the task of conquering the cube.

Monkeypuzzle, I believe they classify this species of tree, its branches expertly supple and slender to preside over whatever remarkable treasure it unearthed at its base. While this object continued to cast a thrall over the buoyant brown ape, Betty-Blue Raygun oscillated on her heel and stalked back to join me: this all eventuated before I might formulate a coherent protest, resigned to the weal of orderly courses of action, understanding that Scotland resented the praxis of reason, knowing reality was infected by the triumph of coincidence here. So it took about thirty seconds. And then Betty-Blue's hands were on me.

To explain:

She cantered back up the aisle, sidled back into the seat I now occupied, my mouth crawling with spidered words not yet born, and then she sank to her knees with some dark ceremony, her eyes strobing with adventurous light, and it was only a matter of leisured limb coordination before I realised she'd eased down my fly with her teeth and was, *mutatis mutandis*, presently inserting her gorgeous face into my pubic growth.

Betty-Blue's mouth yawned with voluminous evil, swallowing my penis so that I swelled inside her cheeks – engulfing my erection while her tongue massaged the tip of the cock – strident in her ministrations such that soon my balls were inflating with heat like a balloon squawed over the spout of a tap as it hisses out a jet of lukewarm water.

This is all highly ephemeral stuff, and unsurprisingly exasperating to describe in retrospect without her fertile mouth here to remind

76

me, but I can declare with a sense of keen observational thrift that I *was* struggling with a charming harmony to prevent myself from howling in paroxysmic abandon as the lady slurped on my shaft, shaving it with her teeth, cosseting me to trigger, and I was just about to invest her mouth with my spunky swill, my heaving gape-breathed body revelling with blood sugar and bermagot, building to a climax that would spray a purple tide of flame from the rushing cave-mouth of me and flow with a verse of lust to the back of her throat, just reconciling myself to the steamy release, the muster of fuck, when she bit me and I yowled. By the time I'd retracted it was all over. I had to blow my load in her astonished eyes, hot spermatozoa all over the seat. She buried her face in my shirt, shaking with mirth, disservicing my blazer to wipe her face. She stunk of patchouli and golden damask. She sounded like lemon pie cooling on the drawn window treatment. We kissed.

✤

The girl's name – though Betty-Blue Raygun was an admirable appellation inasmuch that it captured the hillbilly pageantry of the dear goldplated vixen at her most gregarious and attention-grabbing – was nothing so versified or elemental: she preferred to go by "Per" (as in Persephone) and supposed her surname was "Haven", because that was the honorific of the only family she'd ever suffered the misfortune of unsought gratitude. For, as Per Haven explained it, being recipient to a person's impulse-summoned kindness was the fastest and most strategic method to be left inextricably in that person's debt and so enter into a transaction of ownership in which you were obliged to pay interest to square the tab.

This is why, she persevered, she would never submit to the economics of love. She would end up being in receivership of goods, irreplaceable comestibles like fidelity and companionship, which might never be repaid in full. How might a person feel *comfortable* in a relationship demanding intimacy and emotional disclosure if they were forever persecuted by the auditors of romantic conviction, dogging each candid gesture of bare-hearted vulnerability to ensure you were paying up all that had been originally invested in you? To hear Per Haven tell it, love was the surest way to emotionally bankrupt

77

yourself, for a person never pursued you for love without sickeningly, cravenly, discreditably scheming to obtrude – to mandate – that they be loved in return, for that imperative was prerequisite, *it was only good sense:* you don't invest without expecting to recoup, because love was no socialist free-market, or else it wouldn't prescribe itself to exclusive configurations like monogamy, like commitment. To be a partner in love was to be a partner in business. So Per Haven had learned, through arduous firsthand experience, not to contractually agree – either verbally, physically or otherwise – to actively enter into anybody's debt ever again.

Which is why she was liberated sufficiently to go and inhale some arrogant English stranger's cock on public transport without censorship or the fear that this constituted an act necessitating repayment in the context of sexual commerce. Because Per Haven wasn't after anything resembling love, she could systemically maintain that she was external to emotional or fiduciary obligation. Her joyride blowjobs were only iconographies, mere tokens or ideologues, for the extent to which Per Haven was able to interact with the beleaguered of the world and mitigate their debts without feeling at all needy for like legitimation.

She could hump who she wanted, ejaculate on whoever's satin, swallow your cum or mine, nuzzle a vagina or a neglected dong of unnameable heritage each week without ever going *out of pocket:* in this instance, her left hand was in my very same, vigorously palpating my manhood, but I regained an acuity of mind to snatch her wrist before her fondling became too visceral to object to.

We'd wasted an entire box of mango-perfumed tissues (the Icelander's) to absorb all the jelly-juice I'd consummated onto the back of the chair, and there were still glass-like filaments of semen left spangling the trickiest fissures of the upholstery which I'd grown to accept were irretrievably lacquered to the seat, part of the patchwork now so that only a clean fire could purge the stain. Then we'd initiated our post-coital chat.

There was a startling depth to Per Haven's personality, a vast and chatoyant brilliance, from her tertiary qualifications in twenty-first century literary narratology and sustainable community development, to her enthusiasm for Mexican wrestling and a grave distaste for "amateur theatre", and like I said, she and I would've fucked but she discerned early on that I was a heartbroke English basket-case and it only demanded that I accidentally call her "Pam" a second time for my moral collapse to be any more evident. I needed to clarify my predominant ambition – which was to (a) either get the dodge out of Scotland, or (b) locate a red swan and/or a wrathful Kilmarnock monster – when the words tumbled out of my mouth, in handsome array, thus:

'Have you heard a rumour that a mythological beast roams the paddocks and pastures of Ayrshire? If you have, I should elaborate that I'm looking to conquer it.'

Per Haven's eyes returned my bizarre declaration with amused fascination, her mouth betraying a giggle of milkteeth.

'What could you possibly want with the Lobo of Kilmarnock Downs? The creature's an urban folklore, like the Mothman or phantom kangaroos or Nessie or Keanu Reeves: you can't unequivocally assign even a remote relevance to the unverified allegations which suggest the thing "emerges from the sea" and terrorises the surrounding coastline before baying in the blood of some hundred dead sheep and slipping back into the bay, like a pedant collector of Nazi memorabilia back into a limousine outside Tempelhof. I mean, the whole idea is just sort of... daft. And you're *English!* I thought English intelligentsia prided themselves on the substantive power of rational thought, after pledging promises to learn from that whole Thatcher fuck-up. You weren't an agitator in the Balkan conflict were you? Your daddy didn't work the steel mills, did he, Sebastian? Come home of an evening accompanied by a skulk of pisshead rascals and share blue-collar racist propaganda to you while getting you to hold the telly at a painful angle because the aerial was a scrap of shit and needed replacing?'

'I beg your pardon, you indecent slag –'

'You do look the sort to entertain afternoons strangling stray kittens and hocking flowers retrieved from the local cemetery for a quick buck.' Per Haven was marvelling, with sublime explorations of sadism and comedy, at my violent squirming. She regarded me with a bruised expression, as though my adamant disavowal to laugh at her baity scorn signified proof positive that I was probably the screwloose scrooge she was damning me for being. 'Anyway, there's no reward in investing your faith in the concept of something as spurious as a fucking Lobo –'

79

'You keep saying that word. I don't know what that means.'

'Excuse me?' Per was perplexed: I was irritated.

'That word. "Lobo". Is that an acronym for something exacerbatedly apparent? Large Ogre-like Being Only?'

'Sebastian, it's not an acronym –'

'Land Ocean-Based Octopus? Lava-Originated Badger Orphan? Lemon Oak Body Odour?'

Per grew irate: I persisted. 'Sebastian you've deviated way off course, and it'd just be 94% less complicated if you privileged me with an uninterrupted minute to explain –'

'Local Orange Bald Orangutan?' I blurted, distressingly cavalier and my eyebrows performing steeple vaults into the furthest territories of my ungoverned face. Per Haven perfected a hard open-palm slap across a sweep of my unceasing cheekbones.

My whole head rang with the impact. Blood burned behind my mouth, and pearl-chains of oxygen raced in buoyant symmetries through the reef of my braincoral, like marlin through food-rich waters at the apex of hot season. She'd stopped me in my tracks. I was abloom with startles of colour, and a confronting taste of metal arrested my tongue. I had to gaze at Per the way someone might squint at a distant house occupied by light from within an assault of driving rain. I was thrust into pirouetting around her voltage-sneer like a human moth, I was mesmerised by her courage, I was unseated by her fury.

'Okay, I've shut up, I've shut up. You can spill the beans, and I do apologise. This whole trip has exiled me to batshit country. I think I know what you're going to say. The Lobo of Kilmarnock Downs is troublingly similar to a certain Sir Arthur Conan Doyle beastie…'

'It's not actually a dog, *per se*,' Per said, frowning kindly. 'It's sort of envisioned as a species of giant hyena. Like I iterated prior, you're not going to yield much success attempting to pursue this thing, because the last notarised claim to be afforded any semblance of public and professional speculation around here was about ten years ago when some daft wharfie who vocally fancied himself the last of an illustrious lineage of Scottish pirate, complete with the limp and the ludicrous shanty-speak so archaic and self-proliferated that it defies modern etymology, emerged from the woodwork and alleged that he'd *caught* the fucking thing. How excellent is that, innit? "Anachronistic sea-raider confesses to newspaper to having ensnared legendary monster-hyena in a mud pit of his own complex devising". Aye, I remember the uproar such fallacious folly galvanised in town. Everyone was dead-set convinced that the fella was a certified serial killer, a socially-estranged freak possessing some lurid fascination in Beowulfian romance. And the last I heard, from the perspective of a disinterested spectator, you understand, was that the nautical madman retreated back to the moors and returned to his little citadel on the coast, his rat's-tail between his legs.'

Per shrugged, no longer sustained by my magnanimous assertions that I was in Scotland to overthrow a chimerical scavenger of the lowlands. She narrowed her stare, conflating her brow, winnowing her smile to a single, resentment-whittled point until she generally resembled a duck with an uncharacteristic tuft of polluted plumage. She quacked: 'What in Christ, you man-sized coroner's dildo, is any of this about?'

'What? Me being here in Scotland? Look,' I stammered, fencing with the question until I discerned, through a haggard survey of all withstanding responses to Per Haven's entirely legitimate query, that there was no easy way to circumlocute the irreparably basic idea that who I'd become, in less than a week, was an intimately disturbed man. So I bristled, my knuckles trembling through my hair as I devolved into a state of emotional paranoia and artfully defensive egress, 'Look, I came here to do some study, to avoid thinking about my lost girlfriend, to accompany my friend on some birdwatching ventures, to maybe get laid enough to eclipse a horizon of personal regret.

'But I haven't been able to focus on the PhD, even though I'd be the first to comply or concur that this country's littered with the remnants of peat-preserved bodies like pickled olives scattered across a picnic rug. Plus, and this is a convenient downer for emotional context, my best friend was killed a few days ago. By the chimp,' I confided, shuddering as I succumbed to a reality populated by facts, 'and I feel morally culpable to track down this particular genus of swan to commemorate my friend's last wish, to consummate his dying conviction – and that's led me to this bus-ride in which I intend to find the Lobo, whatever it is. If I find the Lobo, I find the man I'm

81

seeking (which should enable me to secure an easy day-job), and thereon I can commit myself to discovering the swan. See? Also, and this is really increasingly self-evident, but I've got a dismantled skeleton I should bury or dispatch somewhere appropriate because I'm alarmed at the possibility of being incarcerated for theft of someone else's property, and it's only really a matter of serendipitous fortune that I wasn't imprisoned by the troll earlier, because despite all his zeal for linguistics and tropical fish he probably most relishes locking away creeps and disoriented tourists of a questionable tendency. I guess I've been lucky I found you,' I panted, convinced that everything I'd recapitulated resulted in a nonsensical reverie indicative of my warped little worldview, 'I mean it, Per Haven, and I'll disassemble that sentiment by elaborating that if I *hadn't* soaked you with my spunk just now we'd never have engaged in conversation about the reason for my outstanding presence in Scotland. And the fact is I need to locate that same ex-communicated pirate of ill public repute. If you can help me, I will agree to whatever reciprocal request that you demand of me. Just take me to the rat-tailed recluse's hovel, wherever that lies, and I'll regard myself altruistically indebted to you.'

My mouth was full of hot promise, like summer wine. I started to weep, frightfully cognisant that I might die here, marooned in this green country of boisterous hungers so alien to my monarchy of placid, antiseptic Englishmen, and the thought was more than I might bear. O we English had been but fools to risk the perils of Scotland, such exceptional naïfs!

'Just tell me what you'd ask of me,' I gushed. 'Please.'

'Holy shit,' Per Haven gasped, swivelling to keep transfixed, her stare averted, to the water-fouled windowglass opposite her.
'Come on, don't be like that. I'm sorry, alright? Did I unintentionally belittle you? Confuse you? Look, I must just signify an immense twat to you, and if it's any consolation, I find you irrationally sexy. Um. Which is to say –'

'It's not that, Sebastian.'

'Sorry?'

'I'm not dismissing the relevance of your confessions here –'

'What, then? Why won't you look at me? Do I disgust you?' It was all too much; I evacuated my nasal passages messily into my

82

inner-jacket pocket, wailing with bracing gusto. 'Why is everyone so distant here?'

'Sebastian,' the punk-mistress in possession of the wildfire eyes turned to me, and silenced me with her index finger. 'There's a fucking two-headed cow on the road, and it's refusing to vacate the motorway. Do you think we might negotiate our impromptu sex-pact later?'

Bricktop whimpered from the back of the bus. A moment later, he'd knuckled his passage up the aisle and cowered in my lap, my nostalgia overwhelmed by timid mammal stink. He clutched the Rubik's Cube between two cupped paws like it constituted a heart liberated from its frivolous musculature. The bus slowed to a terminal trawl. I heard a cowbell rattle nearby, reminding me of steel mugs against prison bars.

✪

The bus driver, whose plastic nametag suggested was decreed "Finbar Royce Omally" beneath a thumbnail photograph of Henry Fonda sheltering under the brim of a spud-coloured stetson (Finbar shared Henry's alarming sideburns), rotated his ample Scottish frame to confront Per Haven and myself with a wine-tongued gunslinger's pout.

He hiccupped and disengaged from the cab of the vehicle, smacking his lips and crawling like a slug across a razorblade as he succumbed to the idea that he would have to exchange underappreciated dialogue with the freaks congregated at the back of the Stagecoach. As he drew near, accelerating down the carpeted aisle with the laconic wisdom of a fat man whose obesity enhances his physical dexterity and the stealth of his reflexes, Finbar Omally lurched – it's the most precise assignation for the man's favoured mode of locomotion, even if it does stimulate comparisons with a slick shit on a pane of glass – with the propulsion seeming to originate directly from his abdomen, so that I initially interpreted the vision as that of a lean man escorting a self-inflating balloon beneath the sailcloth of his uniform. To surmise my feelings on this extraordinary and inexplicable tableau, it suffices to explain that I was supremely scared – beyond even the fear-reflex activation of my usual squeal function.

83

'Welp, we got ourselves a wee-diddle pickle,' Finbar drawled, inserting an index finger into his left ear up to the middle joint with a vigorous shudder of his trapezoidal face. 'Without's a fella come to collect his retarded calf – I s'pose the term "deformed" is a more politically recognisable diagnosis, but it's not getting to the rudiments of the concern, which is that the cow is fucking *retarded* – and while he's been noncing around the Stagecoach's snout he signalled for me to foist open the front-doors and indulge in a chewy. Now I should forewarn you and assign the relevant context that this fella's a spectacular paragon of moron strangeness, but he holds fast to the deranged opinion that *you*, my peelie-wally, have boarded this bus in an effort to come visit him. Of course, I laboured to deny such nonsense because no intelligent and perspicacious sprat would want to intimate themselves in the company of a renegade cunt, pardon the parlance, that befits the likes of him and his correctly deformed formally retarded two-headed fucking heifer. Still, the contemptible pranny insists that he ain't facilitating a quick blarney with me to entertain my offensive speculations, and seeing that it's probably a porny stretch of the Scottish transport conventions to give free passage to a brass monkey clever enough to crack a Rubik's Cube, I'm resolved to evict you from the vehicle so I don't have to continue exchanging mutt-pedigree doggerel with the nutter and can get back to my sluggish fugue listening to Hank Snow on the box. So to recapitulate, sweetheart, I'm gonna croon to ten in the tenor of B (with the sassy lass, here, offering me accompaniment if she don't mind), in order that you go and debate the cow-wrangling radgie gadgie kook's conundrum on the roadside kerb, amongst the marigold blossoms, so that we might all get to the bottom of this ineffable mystery.'

Finbar Omally's eyes misted over at this juncture, epically encumbered by the gravity of his insight so that his haste and animation appeared to fossilise before our dazzled stares. 'But nowt's so ineffable that it'd injure the value or currency of the "effable", which is why I'm secure in telling you to get the eff off my coach, there's a kinky lad, and fuck off with your lateral-minded chimp, too, if you please.'

What could I say to counter such oratory? Our bloated, scrotum-shaped bus driver with the ranch-hand sideburns and the ambitious

84

sweat stains beneath the pits had me at an intellectual bind. There was nothing for it but to accept that I'd been bested by an eloquent sage of the Scottish commuter tribe, and though he resembled a mutant baby with the features of a future Elmer Fudd, I recognised the epistemological smarts and talcum-sweet generosity of his willingness to give me the benefit of the doubt by supposing that I didn't necessitate a boot in the rectum to get me off the bus. We were both adults here, metaphorically-speaking, and it was only appropriate that I conduct myself with a comparable maturity.

'You mention that this gentleman, with the dual-brained calf, is what we in the frisson of multigendered, transcontinental England refer to as "one or two tube stations short of Barking". May I intrude on your time one further moment to ask why you've arrived at such an assessment?'

Finbar Omally entreated both Per and myself with a slow, candid and tolerant smile. 'He's got a bionic arm, a patch over one eye, and he's dressed in a bin liner, ain't he?'

'Ah, well, capital,' I ventured, resentful of all lunatics though I myself clutched a giant brown ape to my lap.

Finbar Royce Omally yawned with a boozy contempt from behind a hand swimming in fat, the flab-seized extremity concealing most of a morose grin of indeterminate function, and then the man retreated up the aisle once more like a sweating abattoir steak reclaimed by a conveyor-belt.

I watched the chubby charioteer go, at a leisurely trawl, before I returned to exchange piteous glances with Per, contriving to express distress and interrupted admiration, resignation and disarmed dedication to the pink-crested glamourpuss with her trenchant grin, but all the emotional nuances and the barbarous urgency conspired to muddle my face so that I succumbed to a frown the likes of which satisfied a horse with a mouthful of bell peppers perhaps, but not a goodbye countenance to extol to Per my genuine feeling. I felt vindicated in weeping and tried that, but the effort didn't smack of bitter regret so Per requested that I stop. Her exact words were "Sebastian, you look as though you're about lay an egg. Through your throat."

I relaxed, slumping with gratitude, and hesitated before kissing her. Our mouths met, her breath corrupting the integrity of my icy

85

demeanour, so that suddenly I was aflood with her scent of rosewater and red liquorice straws, and I found my fingers interlocked with her own, in a sort of romantic handshake. I would remember Scotland for her, I told her, as the shadows of an arbour of lime trees rippled over her sharp porcelain-ghost face. Per Haven's lips contorted into a plum-coloured sneer.

'Are you going to ask me for my fucking number or not, you Edwardian tit?'

She was a delight, a purple whiskered caterpillar on the lip of your shirt collar, a room vacated of furniture and domestic trappings but startled into occupancy by one thousand dancing asters set astir by a breezeway exploiting a broken window shingle, a gold coin charming the discourteous eyes of passersby at the bottom of a fountain, a cathedral skylight newly unobstructed so that a frieze of immense fantasy was thrust into daylight once more, a butterscotch sundae served in a highball, a blue fish trapped in a coastal rockpool.

Per Haven was all these things, but I was no sentimentalist when logic persisted in intervening so that I might yield to the fact that this was *not* an example of love, insofar that all those analogous visions established this lady-droog with the ugly yet transfixing Depeche Mode coiffure as a fetish beauty, as an *object* to provoke the sublime rather than an authentic emissary for the possibilities inherent of the single white female, this was just a fleeting rendezvous and not a star-fated love, I dare not distort the significance of one toothy blowjob. I let her process my weary nonchalance before she concluded that we'd been caught up in the excitements of spontaneous attraction, but Per did not retreat her offer.

'I'm not overcompensating here, Sebastian. I don't expect us to feel enthralled by future possibilities, by demented yearning. Who fucking knows how this moment will proceed, and I understand you've gotta leg your spidery self into an unusual present, complete with hyenas and pirates. But I might hope we still owe ourselves at least a devastating fuck in the not-so-demanding distance, and perhaps you'll still make me laugh. There's always hope for potential ardour on my end, if the timing's right and you ain't still harbouring a bag of bones around, on public transport.'

This troubled me with feeling, smote me with a cutting affection, scattered my reservations to the furthest scorchmarks of the map,

86

fast enough for me not to over-rationalise my euphoric reaction. I entertained a glimpse to assure myself that our bus-driver had reverted to his loafish repose before his radio of Hank Snow regrets, and then I unsheathed my penis from its Levi enclosure with a jag of my zip-fly, uncoiling the noodle in its half-erect salute so that it weaved and careened before Per Haven's shining eyes.

She was shocked into hysteria, totally consumed by the spontaneity of my farewell, and she mediated this astonishment by covering her mouth in her hands in a venture to prevent giving voice to a blurt of confronted giggles. I jiggled my hips, channelling my expert King Elvis of Graceland impersonation like a Nudie-suit wearing, electric blues-snarling horny mimic of forgotten supremacy, and my cock wobbled up and down with centrifugal comedy, right in Per Haven's face. This may have devolved into pornographic squalor, into feminine discourtesy, into degradation of the female form, but Per was no romantic captor submitting to the diminishing insensitivities of patriarchy at this moment, she was actually just bursting blue with laughter, perfectly tickled by what a moronic goodbye this constituted, what a berserk berk I was grooming myself to seem, and she knew as well as I the inadequacies of my penis, but I had still managed to enthral her with its current performance, which was the very point. She availed my flapping wang with her nose, caressing her septum along the jaunty latitude of the shaft, and we both shared a glance of weary communion, of kindred obedience, a mutual love that neither of us could think to brave explaining which coated our eyes with a longing gleam.

I kept dancing until my cock was spartan of its artful jiggle, and then I just stood before her for fifteen seconds with a limp frenulum, gnawing at my lower lip before whispering with a sneer, "Thank you, thankyouverymuch." She kissed my fly after I'd re-buckled my pants and then I was gone, advancing up the bus, her phone number scrawled in orange lipstick up the length of my forearm. As I disembarked the vehicle, Finbar called out from between two miraculous eyeballs, "What? No encore?" before readjusting the dial of his Hank Snow heartbreak hour.

The doors closed on Bricktop and I, with a ventricle shudder. We waved *bon voyage* to the heavenly face in the far window, as I transferred the fresh sigils scribbled over my wrist into the cheap circuitry of my unremembered mobile phone.

✡

I've known a great many impossible beings in my time, if only because I grew up in the eighties when the very ideological purpose of London seemed to suggest that crazy wasn't merely okay but germane to survival, but though I'm among the first to maintain that there are limited variations of the quintessential oddball's personality type, I am even sure today that I'll never meet someone quite so magnificently demented as Padraig Dunlap.

He possessed a mind of rare distinction, insofar that only geniuses are socially permitted to display such indefatigable paranoia for it to be publicly reconcilable. Make no mistake, Padraig Dunlap was no genius. He was a pirate of the Scottish heath. I was certain of it then, when I capered off the bus with my chimp and overhead luggage, because he swaggered by the roadside with a preposterous limp.

I blinked to shutter my eyes against the warp of daylight cleaving through the lime bowers and swallowed hungrily, the way a crocodile might pant, from within its cylindrical jaw, to convey to a neighbour it was willing to tolerate the company. I could tell that this wasn't achieving the desired effect, but I couldn't be sure that this man communing with two-headed cattle before me wouldn't interpret a more forthright gesture, like a wave or a smile, as a brutal insult against his honour. In brief, he reminded me of the junkies and the racist tramps who conspire and publicly masturbate around the rotten fruit produce in the sewer districts of merchant London. It nonetheless became woefully apparent that to the pirate in his throes of weird animal husbandry I was just some Nazi ballet-dancer lookalike with a chimpanzee in a necktie at my side, so I squinted to ward off the sneer of the sun and shouldered my pack of crumpled clothes and bundled bones against my cooling skin before tilting my head at the fierce celebrity freakshow of Kilmarnock.

'Hello there,' I sang, shuffling to the bank of the road with Bricktop in tow. 'I'm told you are waiting for my arrival?'

Padraig Dunlap thrust out a palm to introduce himself. As I clasped it, shuffling my pack between the blades of my shoulders, I felt my initial discomfort wane and ebb away, my reciprocated grip signifying a meeting of minds (I was at least resigned sufficiently to the truth that I was a strange attractor for feral behaviour, and was as a corollary too raving mad to refute anymore), and there was something about Padraig's searching pupil – its sly twinkle – that simulated a paternal affection.

He basically resembled a hyrax with a highly-evolved taste for theatrical dress, for his face bristled and surfaced from beneath a pelt of coarse, snot-coagulated facial hair and his teeth were all uniformly sharper than most so that he purveyed the illusion of a fiend with a mouth of wicked stockpiled incisors. He ambulated with a limp and that was, self-evidently, because he shunted a hobble-strut of carved redgum rather than a leg, but the substitute's quotidian purpose wasn't to function solely as a peg: in the place of an expertly-hewn prosthetic, Padraig Dunlap sported a pillar of wood which doubled as a *birdfeeder*. It was installed with a fluted hatch of latticed yellow plastic at the knee, and as I stood with profound stupefaction before him, a flock of four chirruping blue finches veered like remote-controlled Jedi pilots through my legs to catch onto the pirate's redgum appendage, before burrowing into the slot retrofitted at the kneecap with a thrash of wing-plumage, before all four vaulted out again with seed kernels seized between their beaks. At any given time, Padraig Dunlap's body would be inhabited by tiny, wuthering interlopers. I was reminded of my hypersensitive episode of fevered thinking in the backpackers bar whilst conversing with Ísleifur, for this time it was an irrefutable realisation that confronted me: this pirate had quarrelling winged body-snatchers exploiting his lower limb *all the time*, day and night.

If this was so conclusively the absolute physical complement of the pirate standing before me, harbouring a triumphant grin, then I may have suffered less prolonged cognitive distress, but the fact was that Padraig also donned an eyepatch of burgundy leather and possessed a bionic arm of sterling steel and fibreglass. He was a scrapheap chimera engineered from junkyard paraphernalia and alloy innovation, a man attired as a pirate but biologically reinforced like an android lunging at the pommel lead of a two-headed cow whilst I stood, passive as an endangered marsupial, blinking with rapid convulsions of the eyelid to visually decode the patent craziness of the present landscape.

89

It was like attempting to blink out a splinter of glass: the image cut that much deeper. That was it; Scotland had unseated me from the rational world. I dwelt, as a jerky, reactive visitor, in a world too wild and unequalled to tame with my underequipped apparatus for sense-making. For the first time since navigating the fantasy of warped and woolly Scotland, I felt free of fear.

This was a land of graceful discovery. I could not reasonably submit to feeling threatened by the dangers retained by Scotland for unwary tourists, because there was nothing to endanger me now that I recognised the country was always yielding worse visions than that which you'd just experienced. It was the result of Scotland's holding pattern: I now understood the lay of the land, and no intervening bump would recognise this newfound synthesis of resolve having claimed my brain, perhaps by locking eyes with my own (I'm steadfast in the belief that they were probably spacey, dilated and consumed by a network of capillaries transmitting integrity-rich messages direct from the pupil along the lines of "This country's finally succeeded in breaking down the ramparts of my sanity"), because he scowled at me with a cryptic scorn, like a joke he couldn't recall the punchline for. His lips withdrew to showcase the naked degradation of his teeth. These were yellow, marbled black, the hue of sweetcorn turds. Padraig Dunlap was grinning at me and there were pterosaurs nesting in his family tree.

'Do they not sell toothpaste or other products promoting the virtues and wellbeing of dental hygiene in this country?' I blurted, inconsolable in my daringly English dismissal of conversational etiquette or verbal decency. 'Almost everyone I've met here seems as disposed to operate a toothbrush as a Brussel sprout is to activate an arse dildo,' I persisted, entirely riddled with disgust by my own conduct. 'You'll be quite unable to chew a mouthful of melon if you exist to dismiss the value of a little cheap sodium fluoride. What I suggest to you, if I can prove this bold, is for you to go to bed each evening chewing on a sliver of soap, and perhaps to keep a spittoon by your pillow for those dribbly *tremens* during the night.' I reviewed my resonating proposal with a grim mouth. 'What am I saying? You'll already have a spittoon beside your pillow.'

I trembled, cognisant of how prudent it proves to keep one's prudish dismay to oneself: you can go around belittling the universe and everything contained in it, but the law of relative spatiality means that nothing you can say to describe another's inadequacies can circumlocute or escape also being applied to you. It pays to be circumspect, to keep your tongue between your teeth. Even if you can taste blood, better that you solicited the spill rather than the fist of a generous interloper. So I summoned my fingers to my pockets and narrowed my eyes against the blare of sudden deep daylight.

'What happened to your arm?' I nodded at the steely positronic piston moulded to Padraig's right metatarsal. 'Did it hurt?'

It was all I could think to say, and it reminded me again how futile and uncooperative the human lexicon is to accurately and efficiently apprehend the hardest impacts of history. I could explain to anyone sheltering an available ear that I harboured a ruptured heart, that there were seconds populated with the phantom bray of Adolfo Cavaggio, days dwelt in goosebumps, death preserved in interlaced lashes. I might fumble my resolve with untoward hands and end up crying, bawling like a newborn, about how much I craved the chemistry of Pamela's vanished body, but like this pirate with the bionic arm I'd jettisoned the object of my person whole millennia ago, before I ever trod my heel on the tarmac, so there's no genius of emotional value to overstate the wages of trauma. All I might need to know was that Padraig Dunlap had once been perfect, unadorned by prosthesis, for only then would it relate to me every hurt you cannot render with language. Only then would I accept that here was a man who knew the unassailable joy of shutting up, and letting your loss do the talking.

'It must've hurt like cactus juice in a cut.' I sniffed, modified my stance.

'Och, it feckin' hurt a long dark dram more than that, aye. It were like havin' me extremity flattened by a deli meat-press, to express the shadow and fire o' the experience. I'd imagine a shark biting your dick off would sting a wee side less. Yessir, I endured myself a very special superheated baptism with the loss of me femur, but I'm fortunate to be privy to an era of discovery and whizzbang technology serendipitously for there to be reconstructive surgeons sharp with the scalpel and clever with the robotic claw design. So I shan't spoil our first intimate moment chewin' your flaps off over my brightest minute of agony because that's not what you've galumphed

91

your sweat-clenched arsehole over dale and dike to consult me fer, aye. So let's talk out our order of business and negotiate 'round this unimpressive foreplay.'

Padraig Dunlap assailed me with a craze-fattened eye fatuous enough to catalyse acrimonious shudders of dark laughter, but I was sensible to recognise the hidden contract underscoring the orchestra of his strange brain-sized eye. He wanted me to ask him, with civil tradition, for a job, as though weary formality were imperative to the privilege. 'Well don't wait fer your scrotum to evolve to do it, lad. Out with the ask.'

I couldn't face the charity, not after all the adversity I'd bested to reach this very juncture, not after all the insuperable drama I'd been compelled to perform alone. 'I want to know what did this to you. Was it a car accident?'

Padraig scowled immediately, jolted by my ugly and sincere curiosity, and he smacked his lips in alarm, to simulate the impression that his face was burrowing into itself with surprising disgust. He had a carbuncular face like Rutger Hauer's, and I almost anticipated that the words "the Tannhäuser Gate" would come bitterly from his lips. Instead, he drolly clicked his tongue against the inside of his cheek with a modicum of self-admonishment. 'Moating did this to me, laddie.'

I blinked, uncertain of the trauma being aired here. 'Sorry? You mean to say you fell into a moat...?'

'Naw, that nowt what I'm expressing. I'm sayin' the moat fell on me.'

I blinked again, my hands scouring my wind-indented hair for purchase: 'Okay, so I'm going to confess to my confusion here, but maybe I don't exactly understand what a moat involves. I was fairly confident that, up to thirty seconds ago, I believed the term described a big hole circumscribed by a ring of rock, yes? Like in Arthurian legend, Shakespearean history productions, the lion enclosure at the zoo? So you're claiming that the *moat*, itself, is actually the physical encumbrance rather than the hole? It's the presence determining the absence and not the other way around?'

This was becoming excessively metaphysical, to a stage in which my hulking grey matter was expected to engage in gymnastic reflection over the philosophical function of being/non-being, and I didn't feel I possessed the true stamina to grapple with the enigma of "when a hole isn't a hole" in my current cagey headspace, so instead I threw up my arms in intellectual defeat.

'Nope, sorry, I just don't get it. A hole isn't what *surrounds* it, that's just prodigious wank. That's like defining an exit wound as the injured body enclosing the bullet-hole. I just can't see how a *moat* can fall on you.'

Padraig Dunlap was well amused by my exasperation because he was balling his fists to his belly and chortling, in trembling frissons of humour, whilst his face became consumed by a rash of pink heat that left him resembling a cycloptic galah with a plume of beard-like spittle dangling from the chin.

'Let me make it easy: the moat is the trough filled with water and it is the ramparts that gird it. The moat's both, just as you can't define an oppositional force without also reinforcing the existence of what it opposes: you got yourself *summer*, fer example, but you can only identify it by the way it pushes back *spring* – otherwise the notion of seasonal division is soddin' arbitrary. So the moat is what you're constructing – the physical channel hewn into the soil's strata – but it's also the stone encircling it to make apparent that what you've engineered ain't just a crop-circle carved into the ground but a functional enclosure from which the individuals elevated at the centre are granted immediate amnesty and protection. A mouth's a hole in your face, lad, but it's also the teeth.'

Padraig gestured to his robotic prosthetic with a bunched eyebrow and coveted a dangerous smile. 'So I was cleaving a ditch in a fierce arc 'round this property inherited by a pennyfarthing earl of some sodden, aphid-mustered sorghum plot when the cattle started mauling each other from base bovine fear and I was proper persuaded to conceive that the fucking Kilmarnock Lobo was back to haunt me, if not the bleedin' mermen out there, with their conch-shells to their ears, conspiring to murder me.' The Scottish pirate's unpatched eye, aglow with psychosis, swivelled to scan the ligature of the coast. 'But it weren't neither of me ole' enemies which spooked the milkers. It were them red swans, all amassed, like Japanese stormclouds, and just as I took a gander the moat collapsed.'

Padraig plundered his pockets for an unknown abundance and retrieved a fist brimming with dehydrated pellets which he duly

93

palmed into the two-headed steer's splayed lips, administering each of the mutated farmyard freak's clattering maws with a mound of the earthy stuff from the inventory of his overalls. The cow honked in chorus, munching contentedly, while its two heads swifted four docile, swimmy eyes to survey me in my vanishing bewilderment, like a harbinger for watchful evil. I competed against my better irrationalities to ignore the creature as Padraig continued with a derelict wheeze.

'The moat suffered a compromise of integrity and piled right onto me left arm, and I could blame the impoverished quality of the loam and peat that I was attempting to sculpt into an embankment but the folly and fact of it is that I was so affronted by the ballsy flock of birds, so startled by their fury and grandeur that I misjudged my purchase on the ditch and sent my spade straight at an untethered rampart of feldspar, about a tonne in density, which struck my arm and sheared the bone from my shoulderblade clean. It was one of the most painful feckin' injuries, in terms of unknowable violence, that I've ever experienced. But I was still rendered voiceless by the swans, which alighted in a congregation onto the other floating base-blocks of feldspar circumscribing the moat, as I squirmed beneath my dreadnought trap like a lepidopterist's prize specimen.

'Aye, there must've been fifty of the cruel, splendid birds. Anyhow, I didn't exalt in much of a moment of spectator's awe for too long because the birds assumed thrust of their diode-sized collective group-mind before erupting from their temporary roost as one, in a thrash of plumage, and whammo! The sudden release of weight sent the fenceline of feldspar tumblin' down on me. The arm was crushed, the leg was distorted beyond repair, and the shock of agony sent me into a white-heat fever until my contractor discovered me moaning my weary suffering from beneath the rubble about a day later.

'This is all some time ago, however, and doesn't bear corresponding reflection. All I know is that the claustrophobia, the physical and anatomical distress, the chill of the icy dusk and the bone-white gleam of cold mineral engulfing my fraying flesh, the empty breadth of my predicament, the vomit cauterising the skin on me cheeks, the pulsing pain populating my brain, the momentum of a quiet and brittle death, it all converged to reveal to me, for perhaps the first time, how *similar* a dry abandoned moat really is to a freshly-turned grave. But I've rallied since, I've been restored my lost appendages, business has cautiously accelerated these past decades into a boom fer our work because of cultural auspice, and I ain't once stopped recalling the sheer red stridulation of those swans despite never having perched a peeper on their fierce form since. And that's where you come in, innit? You're searching for them phantasmagoric cygnets and you need a job. Ísleifur, that thistle-fire Icelandic romantic, lisped a lullaby down the line that you need a fiduciary enema to continue spendin' time in Scotland, and you *need* said time if you're going to exercise some retribution, see those swans, locate that Lobo. I understand your bosom ally died, that he was an unusual geezer close to your gut, and that you refuse to retreat back to Leeds with your plated tail between your reptile pins, so let's discuss the venture at hand, eh? I need a partner, and you fit the fossil record, lad.'

Padraig steered a thumb at the chimpanzee pulling grotesque faces by my side. 'I heard tell that you hated little Bricktop. Fair call if you ask me. He probably pisses a stream on those paws you've been holding.'

I withdrew my chin to my chest, gnawed at my shirt pocket for half a minute. The lime canopy pitched severe frutrient angles, pandanus shadows, wizard symmetries down the line of my arm. I twisted my neck to gaze up into the foliage, some fragile and vulnerable earthling witnessing the docking of a manta-shaped vessel of green sun-glanced polymer over our spurious peopled planet. I stared at the scars banding the branches. In some places, new growth appeared to be spawning with promise from old wounds. A bower of branches like a network of birdfeeder limbs.

'What's the job, Padraig?'

The pirate's face rippled beneath the leather patch. 'Moat reconstruction fer historical preservation. Same as always been.'

I studied the muscle swelling between the man's knuckle joints. I conceded with a snort. 'Okay. I think I can tolerate that. Might even find an opportunity to excavate and examine some bog bodies for the doctoral thesis in the process.' The wind blasted my mouth full of plant spores. I was seized by a spit-fest, grass wands baled between the teeth. 'What the fuck?'

95

Bricktop hunched, guilty and wild with scheming glee, his fingers choked around balls of heather. He blew a raspberry at my dark disapproval, slapped his knee and cavorted around the cow in faun-like delight.

'What do we have here?' Padraig had located a Rubik's Cube at his feet, disbanded because it no longer possessed any interest. I had to admit, he'd exhausted the junky object in record time. 'He didn't even finish it,' Padraig noted, rotating the cube to identify the neglected colours.

'Oh, he finished it all right,' I muttered, clapping the troubled puzzle between my fists, like a half-finished firefly. 'There ain't nothing more to solve.'

✿

My agreement to fulfill the role of assistant labourer – intermediary moat-maker – culminated in a witnessed contract of transliterated Gaelic legalese which stipulated that "if I proved of heathen blood" I would be "ignominiously unsound of principle" not to print and sign my name on the perforation at the foot of the page. There was also some troubling administrivia notated in a sequence of footnotes which appeared to be indirectly concerned with my sexual conduct ("we have to be sure you're a man, you understand," Padraig elaborated helpfully), and my political sympathy for nuclear waste disposal ("that part's just included to stimulate conversation," Padraig observed). Therein yielded one final judiciary clause which was to "comply to all allocated tasks relating to the capture and thorough torture of the Lobo of Kilmarnock," providing we obtained evidence attesting to its existence.

I scrawled my signature on the dotted line.

Padraig Dunlap and I sealed the deal with a reconciliation of palms, grinning together the way of psychologically-unkempt carnies, until the two-headed steer expressed unrest at being used as a writing desk and Padraig removed the contract, authorized in triplicate, from the side of its piebald hide. The beast conspired to present me with the evil eye, all four of them. I thrust my thumb towards Bricktop, whilst yawning with a swivel of the jaw. The chimpanzee skittered a pace away like a shoe-shuffling tramp in a lavender suit. Padraig snorted through the thatch of his nose, deflating slowly.

'What the fuck should I do with the brown ape whilst I'm moating? He can't be permitted to navigate freely through your pasture, here, because he's compelled to react in a bugged-out fever and accost some unsuspecting nature enthusiast. He'll need to be regaled with a watchful eye and unflagging surveillance to ensure the critter doesn't take the plight into pursuing the Lobo into his own paws, as it were. And how do we mitigate against *that* alarming possibility? I can't very well invest all the zeal and precocity you might need on the moat restoration front if I'm having to simultaneously grapple with the best arcane method to inhibit a disoriented chimpanzee from freaking out the public. So that's a bit of a practical conundrum that I wouldn't mind ascertaining an alternative perspective on: do I foist the violent primate back on Ísleifur, or do we solicit someone to do the rabies-sitting?'

Padraig enjoyed that final scrimmage at speedy wordplay because he arrayed his teeth before me with a savage smirk. He held his left elbow in his right hand, as though crossing himself for imminent genuflection. 'I'll do it,' he ventured, his voice advancing through his gullet like a rumble of some anonymous stormfront sweeping closer between canyon walls. 'We'll timeshare the feckin' task whilst we labour over the repair fer the moat.'

I reflected on the offer for an instant, reluctant to authorise Padraig's apocalyptical custodianship lest he fail to apprehend the nuance of looking after Bricktop (the duty would demand that the unhinged primate be distracted *at all times*), but it only obliged a glance at this Scottish polymorph to put all potential unrest to bed.

Of course Padraig could cope with the chimpanzee's ceaseless appetite for bedlam! A moat fell on him and he came out the other side equipped with the arm of a Schwarzeneggerian cyborg. He might not possess an expert insight into the anthropological curiosities of brown apes, but Padraig could hold his own. There was a cerulean gleam in the chrome of the pirate's alloy appendage which seemed to suggest that Padraig could present tiny countries beneath the cloche to expectant diners without an expended bead of sweat or fleeting expression of strain: the bionic arm could absorb the impacts of any grave weight and still respond with the patina glint of one fucking

97

strong unit of iron biceps. Bricktop might chafe at the reins but the pirate's gauntlet-hold wouldn't slacken. So I hesitated no longer, and forged the bargain with a leer which best exhibited my eyeteeth.

'So you'll have to presume I'm an unvarying imbecile and explain to me what a moat is, and how you restore one.'

Padraig Dunlap exhaled, making the sound a foot makes when it's thrust into a molehill of moist dung. 'Well there's a fond coincidence,' he rumbled from beneath his crimson eyepatch, 'I already take you for an unvarying imbecile, so we're leagues ahead already.'

And so my tutelage began. I was instructed to follow Padraig with a fidelitous ear, while surmounting and cloaking the landscape with my chafing shadow, and as we strove ever higher over sweetgrass and tumbledown peat with our shins assuming a ruckle of moss-veined shit through the blue glades I found myself grateful to possess a heartbeat, however twee or Taoist that sounds, because it was gracing me with an experience of the world. I watched a robin monopolise a fencepost in his gangster finery, a quarrel like a tommygun rat-a-tatting from his throat. Locusts scissored through the underbrush, like musical thorns, leaving vague stings on the periphery of my flesh. A surly old ewe, it's face a cankle of wisdom and dismay, offloaded a few kilograms of foul waste over an imperceptible incline, and I waited to observe if they would roll like rock or collect like cones at the base of a pine. The faeces did neither: it glistened like jelly emerging from a can and, as if to mock my comprehension of the arithmetic of rural living and everything my nostalgic folly signified, it *ran* through the tussock like river water. The brown slurry described a clef over the hillslant, and I had to confess that there was a music there, even in the evacuation of bowels, because the wilderness existed at the domestic sphere of wild creatures: the quotidian could be beautiful too, in the right environs. Who was I to debate the way a wilderness should captivate? Inasmuch as I could concede, a defecating sheep was exactly the right type of "wild" a dismally-unacquainted Englishman could expect, and there was certainly no more unforgiving a beast than Padraig who sneered at the stink and then bellowed:

'What I wouldn't give to live someplace less populated by wildlife and smelling so morbidly of barnyard methane! Makes you want to

98

clench your neck between your knees and whimper your way to a world less consumed by the evils of nature.'

I stood behind him momentarily perplexed and unreciprocating, boggled by the arcane reality that Padraig Dunlap was uncharmed by the splendour and purity of Scotland's untamed environment. But then I stepped in a turd and I had to admit a hasty allegiance.

'Do you ever question your calling the same way? I mean,' I vacillated, applying a stick to the underside of my refined suede in an effort to lever off an auspiciously vigilant cowpat, 'you react against the moors and the highlands with elegant disgust, but if I possessed such stark disdain for the outdoors as it's evident you do, I would consider separating, manoeuvring and arranging stone for hours at a time as the terminus of nature-spun horror. How can you possibly *stand* moating? I have to imagine you were once a nautical man, or at least intrigued by the promises of the sea, so how the fuck did you end up devoting yourself to a calling so drearily landlocked?'

Padraig was bestowed the countenance of a popeyed mandrill, and here he disinherited himself of all jungle bile by collapsing into a sharklike yawn which soon softened the damages of his face. He smacked his lips, as if to welcome the wetting of said whistle.

'Aye, you're a beaming lad, eh, a wise weasel of Brittany, and I respect your intelligence (though its intention so frequently appears to function as a method to disarm thy neighbour and train him beneath the star of the moron constellation), but because you ask I will address. To wit: I loved the feckin' ocean, its white swathe and the trillion gilled yahoos, with their swift wings, slicing over coral and carving into jetstream curtains. There are so many awesome fish in our world, Sebastian. Your armpit would bleed to compute the varieties. Here's a clue: when I was bound to my ship, a prawn trawler, fer the eighteen years it demanded of my calendar whilst my face transferred its most pink and young components to the purple blaze of the long and lasting catch of water – an elastic habitat to dwarf the sun – what I craved most was to hear *voices in the waves*. Excuse the schizophrenic desire, and understand: there ain't nowt beyond the prow of a merchant vessel to keep you company but the boom of pelicans squabbling over squid gut, and that vacant cave of friendless static, a sea-hiss that corrodes the radio in any tired man's brain, it can excite grave tastes.

99

'What I remember most is awakening to a pang fer company. I began seeking patterns in the vocabulary of the closest fish. If a bream or a perch or a pilchard or a bass revealed its iridescent stomach on the decks of my clipper-ship, whilst crewmen fustered and flapped below the wheelhouse with their buckets and tridents to parse the bycatch from the clustering glut of prawns we heaped onto ice, I would elevate the piscine interloper to my eye and watch it strive to communicate through the burden of air and without a tongue to manipulate language in an endearing or persuasive way.

'I might pretend to be extracting an agonised farewell kiss from the vaginal beak of that deep-sea denizen, but what the guffawing onlookers with their heaving shoulders failed to discern was that this twisted intimacy existed to promote an exchange between species; I was assuming an endeavour of new science and parlance. I was like Jack Pallance. I spoke very seldom and only in whispered answers. I learned to ululate, to palliate, to undulate my mouth muscles. I schooled myself in trampling language between my teeth, in straining to elocute as if I were haggling beneath densities of pressurised seawater, the exact variables which would efface the dialect of the deep from producing sense in our ears. I was an exponent of fishspeak.

'I sliced transversal cuts in my neck so that no-one would know, deep perforations with a cautious blade. I took to wearing a scarf in the eyeshot of the crew, red as throttled Mexico, but eventually I lost too much blood and I was compelled to repair the folds of fat beneath my chin, zip up the gills with stitches. The qualified medic located me below deck, fevered from bloodloss and unsterile surgery, with a clat of whitebait peeping out from between my lips. He later informed me that I had been struggling to coerce the fish to lay eggs in my lungs, so that I might yield to the freak nature of the sea and abandon my body to the needs of the reef beasts. I had hoped they might mutate my anatomy and allow me to adopt the tongue of the ocean mass with fluency. Perhaps they might erupt through my doughty white chest, gift me with fins, with scales, with webbed spines, pixellated flesh.

'I'd gone mad as an Ebola-contagioned wingnut. Poor devil, I'd swept my marbles into all exits, down all gaping stormdrains. When they escorted me on land, with concerned frowns, I was certain

100

I would not make it to the rear of the flickering ambulance, that I would choke from the water retreating beneath me feet. They'd fashioned a hook to my jaw, featherweight but talon-cruel, and they were reeling me in to lobotomise my gasping skull, fillet my hanging bits from scrotum to lip. Put me in the bed, seized and prostrate, my wrists locked above my ears and my ankles spreadeagled to derange my form, a tube inserted through my nose the way you suck out the guts of a mussel with a straw. A starfish lunatic; an echinoderm split to its axis. The doors closed at my heels and inquisitive men monitored my breathing in spectrograph changes, congregatin' around devices that reminded me of echolocation boxes. They were mapping my body fer movement. They were after my final minnow of rancour.

'When I came to, I was instructed to sit interviews with case-workers, psychoanalysts, neurobiologists and doctors to pinpoint my psychosis. This persisted fer months, until the cocktail of pharmaceutical brain-chasers affronted us all with a notable success. I no longer hallucinated. I barely disagreed or disobeyed. I merely believed myself to be a pirate, and I'd been sponging up the state's medical and fiscal benefits fer long enough for this metamorphosis to account fer success. I was decommissioned from the hospital facility on the provision I continue administering goofballs to myself and came to appreciate that I would be refused, by government auspice, all future work that directly or inconsequentially implicated the industry of Scottish fisheries. So I forgot my pact with the sea, in time. I came to relish the unvaried support of earth beneath yon toes.

'For an aeon, porkchop, the weight of the exile felt too much like embracing a falling wall. Availing yourself of intellect and scrabbling, a dark-planted stooge, to defend the sprawl, to salvage a collapse. I may as well have caught bullets between a molared grin for the surly content of fundamental carnivores, spectators craving bloodloss with their vaudeville. I may as well have fed letters of untame escape through the invisible squeezes of an ice-brick wall, fer all my fumbling and hatred.'

Padraig indicated the alien lope of the two-headed steer crunching up soft, devoured green earth in front of us, gesturing with a squint and a rotation of the shoulder. He seemed devastated in the model of storybook heroes, plaintive in the trail of a cape that bunched into impossible configurations when a stirring breeze stole by. Broken by the negligent affections of an ocean as dark as a scrum. A look of pain assailed him for a second, an old wound reactivated by scorn, and he squared his jaw like the cow we escorted.

'It's not always possible to love something enough to encourage its banishment from mind. Aye, sometimes it's like admitting defeat to a dead friend.'

I scowled, my mouth overwhelmed by the taste of bitter brine, and I burrowed my eyes into my knuckles. Gave them a troubled polish.

'So I guess moating developed as an outlet for your grief, a discipline you could bury yourself in, so to speak, heaving generous bluffs of rock into the accurate formation to *block out the sea* at every brickturn of geometry.' Now it was the pirate's chance to scowl, to clench his metal fingers, to darken the stark of his brow. 'I'm willing to observe the standards and lanyards of the trade, here, Padraig, but I came to find my own peace of mind, though I loathe that phrase for its synonymy to "fragment of brain", of which I'm probably needing to locate anyway. It's actually *resolution* I'm referring to – the promise of a finite absolve, of a gleaming closure. That's why I sought you out.'

Padraig stormed behind a well-behaved jaw, abbreviated my cowlick-rasped melancholy with a puckered sneer of the lips. He didn't want to engage me on this concern, not least because it implicated a recent history of celebrity disregard, of travestied honour, of paparazzi betraying his pleading claims with mocking lens-caps and squandered snickers. He didn't want to face facts, live up to the music, make amends with his status of folly, reconcile his fantastical testimony with the detest displayed him by the cruel gatekeepers of legitimation. He didn't even want to remember the dismay of a recent yesterday.

'You refer, of course, to the sodding Lobo, eh? You want to avenge yourself on this beastie's kingly head.'

'I want to kill the thing, yes,' I confided, with a weird conviction, as though this had already presented itself as a foregone conclusion. If my eyes had strobed red to ultraviolet to white and I started singing snakes to my bootlaces so that pythons circumnavigated my pelvis and fashioned me a crown I would not have been alarmed. Someplace, external to my direct scrutiny, I'd become the little corn-wine boy who sailed kites at night, who kept the devil on speed-dial.

'The fact is, Padraig, that I pursued Ísleifur's yawn of a goosechase so that I might ensnare the Lobo, and kill the fucking monster. I apologise if this confession prompts you to reassess my employ, because I know you'd inflate with *gravitas* over the possibility that I might genuinely seek to restore moats. So I'm sorry if I haven't been transparent during this exchange, but what I'm looking to do foremost is eat the fat, warm heart of the evil creature that murdered my friend. Scotland's a remarkable realm of sly coincidence, but I didn't agree to take on the role of caretaker to a paranoid chimpanzee, nor ignore the likelihood that you became psychologically unhinged while on the open seas, if not to wrangle a satisfaction of my own devising. I can accept all the peculiarity of my present situation, but I harbour a greed for the death of that Lobo, whatever the fuck it is.'

My hands became balls, but not the sort for playing; my ears hummed, as if I'd emerged from the inside of a helicopter. 'There's the rub: I can't say what it is, or how viable these statements of excited witnesses are until I *see* the thing myself. So I'll cut right to my ultimatum. Either you propose a method of capture, or I walk and dissolve the contract I just signed. I'm afraid you'll have to take me at face value, here, or my name isn't Samwise Gamgee,' I brayed, wild atop our slope, while gesturing to the contract clutched to Padraig's chest. 'For a lark,' I explained.

'But it's not even your name!' Padraig Dunlap barked, a sour and gruff old Robocop with feeble nostrils. 'This is signed in absolute perfidy! How can I conduct business if you ain't even willing to be honest with a potential employer! For a bleedin' lark, he says! Commits forgery on a legally-binding contract that I've beneficently prepared without recompense, and the pliant pillock with his tweedy deceit tells me it's all just a feckin' lark!' Padraig was rifling violently through the documents, his mad old eye racing. I watched him ascertain the degree of my ironic application. 'Who the bald scrote is this Samwise Gamgee? I'm at a total loss, you little arse marmot.'

'Uhuh, not a reader I see. Fear not – he's one helluva manservant,' I chided, shifting my weight in a plot of moss, with a palm visoring my

103

eyes. 'Which is what I'll be, cross my gallant English heart, providing you maintain your arse of the bargain and bring me the Lobo.' I sighed, and returned to wrestle pupils with Padraig's testicular only. I threw up my hands, tired of cross-cultural diplomacy. 'You do this for me and you can regard me as your supernumerary, Padraig. I'll even sign your sodding *arm*.'

'What? The way some vagrant of the feminine caress has scrawled all down yours? Or is that your own lipstick on show?' Padraig froze, his vision in the middle distance, a tentative warrior divining the geology of his green hastened country. He harkened, expression freshly vivid, and launched a finger past my disquieted back. 'What in hellfire?'

'Now, look, Padraig, I'm not going to play sucker to your ruse –'

'Your freak monkey has a fucken skull in his paws!'

And sure enough, with a languid poetry of water purling around a horizon, as I twisted to indulge the pirate's raucous allegation, I watched Bricktop recreate the scene from Kubrick's *2001: A Space Odyssey*, but this particular envisioning involved the brown ape going frantic around my forsaken satchel. His paws drummed appendages belonging to Vasquez against one another in percussive frivolity. He was engineering a xylophone from the skeleton's dismantled wreckage. There was something daringly Shakespearean about the re-enactment, but then he revealingly levered Vasquez's skull beneath his feet. With a simian yodel, he crushed the cranium. At that moment I came harrying down to contain him, but Bricktop had already loosened hell from its brazen gate. The fear on the hyperdriven chimpanzee's visage told me all I burned to know.

I careened over thistle and peat-moss, unearthly fungus knuckling up from the purest spirals of cordite-black soil, my once-gloried and enviable Jack London heels cavorting in the minor explosions of Scottish spores, my feet powdered in orange lichen as if to liken their leather to gold felt, shoes fashioned from fedora hats for angelic soles. I ran; you could have played the electric harmonies of Vangelis down hillside and glen, you could have mistaken Sebastian Sackworth as the courier between gods and men.

It would not have represented a peculiarity of perception for a watchful shepherd to interpret my descent as the arbiter for a forthcoming onslaught, for I was blue in the face like I was painted in woad, and my hair abandoned its uncanny augmentation, so that it flamed red as though a skull trailing tiger flax into the yellow silence, and if you were clever you'd consign the vision to the abundance of orange powder distributed by my descent, but there was also a spectacular melodrama to my wrath. I belted beneath the decay of our day, and Bricktop resigned himself to my supremacy by thrusting his endangered face into the sanctuary of his blue blazer.

He was as timid as a seahorse. The fact was, Bricktop was saturated in brains. Blood, juice, mind-meat and cerebrospinal fluid was trickling in rills of human foulness from the sleeves of his jacket. The chimp was inanimate with trauma, consumed by a fugue state of desperate quiet. He shuddered beneath his topcoat with giant dramatic eyes, unprepared for the repellent consequences of his hyperanimated play, reduced to a mess of disfigured mammal soaked to the bone with wretchedness.

I was gobsmacked; I hunched, panted bracingly, surveying the chaos with bewildered reflexes. Vasquez Duchamp, my skeleton stowaway, now strew before my wet gaze in a riot of old cueball-coloured bones. I sifted the scatterings with a fastidious toe, feeling a resolve to prevent a spontaneous nosebleed, and the accumulated osseous relics clattered and rasped against themselves, the bones of limbs and ribs colliding in the way of confetti inside a kaleidoscope.

For a time, my belly still burning with acid disgust, I listened to the susurrus with a clouded brow. I could only compute the obvious: Vasquez had been real all along, which is to say a corpse rather than a simulacrum, which is to recognise that when you're too close to an inevitable fact it's more challenging to reconcile with that evidence, which is to say that I'd been shouldering a dead body around for *days now* without comprehending the repercussions. I wanted to cuss, for I could have been imprisoned, interrogated, tortured, forgotten to rot the way of Vasquez, the corpse I'd dismantled, the body I'd defaced.

And what simulation of anthropology enthusiast was I not to discern a cadaver from a mannequin when I was ornamenting its rotting scalp with a beret of poor taste? How *could* such a momentous

105

truth evade my expert reckoning? How staggered was I to surmise that I'd been angsting over bog bodies for the entirety of my Scottish marooning, when there languished the perfect specimen right beneath my nose under the artful guise of an egalitarian skeleton? I could not calculate the neglect!

I was a grandiloquent wanker, but it unsettled me to understand that everything that had transposed since retrieving Vasquez from the gullet of the buffalo had been coloured differently than I had interpreted it: more succinctly, I'd been escorting a dead human in calcified armour throughout the cold climes of the Kilmarnock coast for too long for it to be either psychologically stable or criminally respectable, and my book-bothering erudition concerning *corpus delicti* had accounted for no proven academic realisation.

I'd disembodied a corpse, disassembled its pale parts and jumbled them into my side-satchel, and idled my time in the company of others with a ubiquitous equanimity that I had a *dead man's bones* sinking into my back.

Porter of the necropolis! transportation agent for the vertically-challenged! more hearse than man! a terminal creep with a fetish for the defunct and the exsanguinous mass! a have-corpse-will-travel defiler of the sweetly surrendered! Perhaps this is who I'd always been, perhaps this is who Pamela disowned and deserted, perhaps *this* is what Bricktop, even Ísleifur ascribed to my foppish behaviour and esoteric mode of dress.

I was emotionally-unavailable, albino-hued, rarely dishevelled and seamlessly arranged, dry and caustic, belittling and barometric, tall and waning like a chocolate pencil, quick to react and fond to fuck, with a crowded frame like a mortician shunting cadavers. It would not be perplexing to envision me a killer. And yet I could not pretend that this notion disarmed me of every achievable intelligent reaction. To stand squelching in brain matter expedited matters of the moment: I vomited in my palm, a hiccup of yellow funk that taffied off my fingers like I'd just delivered a baby giraffe one-handed.

I lurched to the earth and extinguished my burning hand on the grass, wiping off the rancid gristle. Bricktop murmured morose reminiscences in a penitent state of trauma. This fucking monkey has seen too much of the world, I thought. I wanted to bawl.

Padraig hove into view, a one-eyed dwarf on his last legs. He heaved and snarled, sputtering into a hulked fist, blood raging to his brain as he continued to pant from the downhill pursuit. I watched him collapse on a placid verge of sweetgrass, his positronic forearm acting as a fulcrum while he narrowed his gaze and widened his mouth. We all reclined, our silhouettes carving against the sun on the hill, each one of us lusting for a pretty breath.

We were tattered by haste. Our panting tongues cooperated to retreat beneath the advance of light. The sun was setting without bravery or charm. It was all too broken now. I could imagine years passing and still dwelling in a shadow of shame, regret and skeleton disarray. If I knew a way forward, if I could intuit a chance at high valour, it had all been assaulted by the scent of decay prevailing on the breeze.

Padraig winced, punishing my silence with a hefted finger. 'You've got orange lichen all in your bloody hair, lad. You look as if you've been soddin' favouring a *mushroom* fer a pocket-comb.' Padraig was a mocking ocular, a starved eye sweating for a bite. He dismissed the heartbreak and mystery of the skeleton predicament with a sigh through his nose. 'So you were harbouring a bag o' bones I see. Extraordinarily piratical of yon, Sebastian, you gold-plated vermin of Brittanic shores. What I might inquire – if I were to be monstrously indiscreet or intrusive – is what a cockamamy scoundrel such as befits the Sackworth ilk might desire from such horror. Does ritual disembodiment float your feckin' boat, lad?'

I whimpered, transferred my guilt to my fingertips, transfixed myself by guessing the possibilities for my hands. Maybe I was intended for finer veneration than fossicking for research gold amidst the bloat of fever-slain bodies. There was probably a repressed rationale as to why my doctoral thesis was progressing nowhere: if I picked up a pen, I wasn't certain what would come out.

'I had no idea,' I whispered, tears freewheeling on the slick of my vision. I spat and sobbed, 'Look, comprehend that I've gone through a gamut of difficult circumstances since arriving in your fucking country, and the *whole* time I had no cognisant or conflicted idea that this assemblage of human detritus was any more authentic than the jigsaw remains of a glow-in-the-dark puzzle dinosaur! But now that I do, I'm extremely scared. Christ, Padraig,' I swallowed, huffing

107

bubbles through a mouth of hot grief, 'what the fuck do I do? There was still physical *brain strata* in this deflated skull! The fucking ape knew it – he may have knew it all along! I could've been implicated as an enormous cunning-shun twathole murderer!'

'Oh, I think, in the context, that "implicated" is rather a romantic phrase for the terminology used to assess your involvement, if a fat fuck of a vigilante police had interrupted you shoulderin' a sack of spare corpse parts during your merry travels.'

'Thank you for clarifying my confusion, Padraig,' I seethed, 'I can honestly identify where the recontextualisation benefits my present issue. You've graciously helped in suggesting *fuck knows what* to dispense with the scattered fossils of death littering the damn hillside!'

I waved my hand to indicate the final clutter of a collapsed Vasquez Duchamp. I heard something, perhaps an elbow joint or cheek, crunch underfoot. I succumbed to sobbing and stepped on a few more musical ends, my head shaking between the fat of my hands.

'What the blarney are you doing now, genius! You're stepping on the sorry fucker!'

This much was true, but still I marched in a disassociated haze, grinding dispersed toes and teeth beneath the heels of my searching shoes. At every sound, with each hollow crackle or offensive break I whined a little higher, a little more remorsefully. A kneecap rattled, a jaw-part crunched. I cried, I cried. A spinal segment chafed, a rib column whipcracked. I gurgled, I trilled. Eventually Padraig Dunlap just had to shoulder-barge me to the ground, and apply his alloy fist to my testicles to prevent me from persisting in my heavy-hearted destruction. He levered an unfriendly rivet-studded knuckle into the cleft between my gonads and shifted his weight. This seemed to do the trick. The percussion was replaced by vibrato.

'You sound like a swan,' he jibed affectionately, momentarily awash in the clarion drone of my falsetto screams. 'I know you're not an amateur ornithologist like your bosom sod was, so I'm ambiguous about how much you *care* when it comes to birdlife, but it's an interesting fact that people summate the song of a swan as that of a "honk". It ain't honky-tonk at all – it's more discordant than that, like a biophony performed by a doo-wop band, and it throbs through your cochlea with the warfare of a rainforest chorus. You always hear daft *blather* about swans communicating in honks, but it's more similar to boogie-woogie, to a bolt from the landscape of blues.' Padraig sighed, dissatisfied with my one-note reaction to his tutelage. 'Sodom and Begorrah, you don't quit your tremblin' solo for anybody, do you?'

Padraig was wearily correct, and because this signified no authentic intellectual triumph – I shouldn't have to convince anyone at this point of my delight in whining – he duly withdrew his pressure-hold on my royal English balls.

He yawned, and threw up his arms. 'You're silent because you're chilled by the idea that you disregarded a dead man when he was right in front of your kisser, am I right?'

I gulped, and nursed my scrotum, with perhaps slightly more decorum than Bricktop (who did the same thing). To be honest, it wasn't a qualification I'd maintain if pressed. 'I think it might be wise if I just returned home,' I ventured, unfeelingly, examining my resolve. 'I mean, this has all scaled itself much larger and more extravagantly than I'd intended. I'm not even sure how I came to be entangled in such scandalous cheer as all this. Let's clock it off at the skeleton, shall we, the unidentified corpse, and I'll slink like a fractured lizard back home. Oh for a future of hot-buttered toast.'

And then I wept again, with gusto.

Padraig gloated merrily, his fists on his hips, affording me all the disapproval and spleen he could muster through the vehicle of a crimson eyepatch. His throat expanded to recall a muddy-eyed coelacanth at the height of trilobite season.

'You're a vain piece of work,' he grinned. 'Christ Almighty, it's a marvel anybody ever let you keep those tearducts. Look, I've formulated a *plan.*'

I bellowed through the visor of snot and murky pores, avenging myself on the prospect of a convenient redemption. 'What are you referring to, you strongarmed metal-handed mental-case? The more you enjoy yourself, the creepier the *Blade Runner* flashbacks! Out with it, man!'

'You've desecrated and grifted the enduring honour of your skeleton consigliere, here, drawn Errol Flynn moustaches *and* swastikas over the reaper man's just-cooling chassis of rag-and-bones –'

'That was just the one swastika!'

'— and you've exploited the possibilities for an earnest, go-for-broke burial to reconcile your loveless designs many times over, instead opting to transport a deceased participant in the Grand Human Event with nuffin more decent than a fucken zip-bag of stench-ripe old clothes –'

'Oh, come on, now. It was all I *had*, wiseguy –'

'— and you allowed a notoriously paranoiac chimpanzee to muster access to said satchel and violate the deceased remains across the wides of the sodding Scottish countryside, without any preventative precaution put in place –'

'Oh, go fuck yourself and your alliteration!' I sobbed.

'— so now's the time you wrangle the chance to send him off with a hero's commiseration like the vanquished legends of Valhalla, or feckin' Færie, you see.'

I blinked; exploded with guilt. 'How do I do that?' I mumbled.

'We use the begotten bones to bait the Lobo, of course,' Padraig beamed.

I had to admit, Vasquez would do us proud in the jaws of a freak hyena.

We set out to coerce and trap the Lobo of Kilmarnock over the following week. During that time, Padraig Dunlap extolled upon me his scholarly approach to the craft of moating, always advising (and occasionally hectoring) me in subdued Gaelic tones, and I was no longer consumed by self-repudiation at my violation of Vasquez, I enjoyed the soft posture of the land and its geography by the sea, I did not think of Pamela rising out of bed alone or in company, I remembered my pact to intimate myself with the pleasures of the Scottish landmass that I honoured Adolfo by renewing, and stone seemed to fold like bread beneath my touch.

The pirate and I rolled, savaged, heaved and winched hundreds of beach-stone, granite, cinder clay and gypsum blocks over the duration of the week, and when the haul was complete, our chests summoning happy dread to our eyes, we would collapse on the black exact hills, leaking out the week, and the night bathed us in a cool tonnage of pleasing air. By day, we would construct our moat.

The grand scheme was to engineer a refuge for Padraig's cattle and sheep, before committing ourselves to reassembling Vasquez Duchamp on a stake, arranged like a crucifixion, and bloodying him with boar guts and fish offal. This was a method owing to the art of chumming which Padraig had perfected on the animal seas. A pit with lubricated sides would be excavated, but as a precaution for the Lobo's size and splendour, the gulf would have to function less like a trough and more similarly to a desert well. We would conceal the opening with a grass lattice, but reinforce the cover's centrepoint to support the weight of a shark heart which would hulk and bleed as it defrosted less than a handspan from actual levitation. At the bottom of the well would be affixed great blades designed for filleting mako and marlin, and these we would sharpen and hone over hot coals. Our intent was to capture and ensnare the Lobo, madden it with injury, but avoid killing it without first entitling us with the victory of witnessing the monster thrash and suffer for all its primal romantic evil.

We were not hateful executors, because there was less repugnance than easy sophistry in our mutual giggles, our bedevilled grins, and we did not commit our meticulous act motivated by an engine of subzero revenge. We were after its *apology*, not its protracted or belaboured agonies. I could not pledge what it is I might confront – whether the Lobo was more similar to a wolf than a prairie hound in physiognomy, in bright wild array – but I wanted to know that it grieved over its choice to threaten my schizophrenic chimp. Could I expect more than a gall-charged woundedness, an aggrandized retaliation, a pounce for the warmth in my throat? Could I really hope to bully remorse from a mass-murdering highland predator of myth and fire? Well, no: I try not to pretend to be stupid, though I can't obliterate such an interference intruding between my voicebox and my mouth on infrequent occasions, so I'm compelled to confess to my follies. Fact was, I knew the Lobo wouldn't furnish me with any promised apology. But what a man soon learns, when wielding dolphin-cutlet knives, is that it's practically worth it just to try and earn one.

Each morning I would awaken to the sound of birdsong – it would rouse me from vanity or depression or inert disgust with the matrices of human choice, just before I shambled before the plate

111

of mirror-glass and experienced a minor lapse of emotional *déjà vu* – and the tune would electrify my waking brain, some articulation of strident, urgent, familiar music, I would feel conscious of my connection to a braver force, a more elegant life, then pancakes would swim down my aesophagus and yesterday's breakfast would escape through a sewer downpipe. *The circle of life*, as the shaman baboon would suggest. For the first time in my life, I felt natural, complacent in my mortality, *rural.*

One morning I started to consciousness, navigated my way through our encampment of accumulated rock, and stood aghast.

The sun was metastasising the terrain, lasering the slopes and burrows a magnesium red; my shadow discovered a backdrop cinema for the use of its immensity; I summoned my shoulders to my ears; I pleasured in slackjaw reverence. A tide of locusts, seething in tanks of wild armoury, plundered the hill of its domestic modesty. They exploded through the seasons, exhibiting the vivid gallantry of orange autumn maples, white winter hibernations, verdant spring flowers, xanthous summer décolletage – colours that screamed across my vision, and I had to ward my mouth to avoid partaking of an uncooperative breakfast while the whooshing exile of fleet cantilevered wings trimmed the hair on the backs of my forearms. The locusts swarmed through me, obviously convinced of their supremacy, and when I'd fallen to my shoulder spitting dismembered legs and chitin, I saw them gather fury and escalate into one famous, shifting, tessellated mass, change direction like a dance, and retreat to the sea before I slumped abandoned, crazed by intensity. They left me with the ghost of Adolfo Cavaggio one final time. I could hear the laughter, down below, booming on the rocks. It was a gorgeous melancholy, a dead friend twinned with nature.

'What in the church's vile name was that? Sounded fucken supernatural, that did.' Padraig scowled at my spreadeagled leisure, savaged by the jostling of the plague.

'Sorry, that was me,' I blurted, 'morning aerobics of the musical kind.'

'Christ, lad,' Padraig frowned, yawning, 'your farts sure do sound a lot like a locust plague.' Then he writhed in his knapsack and went back to sleep.

When he finally did stagger from the wreckage of bed, and only after he swilled a mug of piping lamb tea through his moustache, Padraig clenched his metal fist, restocked his pipe with tobacco and commenced his oration from the stoop of a basalt pillar.

'Today,' he revealed, brightening, 'we build the fucker.'

And without egregious ceremony, or distorted expectations, build is what we did. Our architectural schematic was charted in dirt and would instruct the literate passerby with an appreciation for tiny maps scrawled between dung piles that our overarching objective was to construct a *castle keep*. Inside the central antechamber of the keep would mill Padraig's migrant sheep population and the one or two deformed cows he could show for his travails to make a feasible living from the land, as resistant and engulfing as it was. The animals would be protected by a stone annexe that described a walled circumference around the inner chamber, so that the indignant herd was enclosed from sight of the world. They would have an elevated platform or plateau of grass to graze on, and at night we would alternate the duty to keep watch over the lethargic community of ungulates while Bricktop was entrusted with a large, indiscrete, shrill towncrier's bell which we instructed him to rattle if the Lobo thwarted our trap. The chimp assumed vigil from a solitary beech tree, from which branches he dangled, lumbered and scarpered. Around the immediate radius of the keep would be gouged our moat, a circular ditch excavated with threatening precision, in which a causeway of water would separate the keep from direct exploitation and which obstructed land-access in the situation that the Lobo caught an incidental whiff of something it seized a smug hankering for.

The moat would occupy a thirty-five metre wide circumference and an entire month of ardent, haemorrhoid-specific toil, but Padraig ensured that the backbreaking, tedious, depraved labour would proceed with an enchanting alacrity providing that I thrilled in listening to the intricate history of his lifelong hatred of mermen, newspaper journalists, prosthetic adjustments, untrustworthy prostitutes, and Jamaican fruit ("now there's an entire society convinced of the value of clammy, sour melon!") In fact, the venture appeared to approach completion in no time at all – or at least a vacant catatonic period consisting mostly of abstraction and foul

113

mutton dinners – and there *were* transcendent days in which it felt as though all Padraig and I achieved was to sit in gargoyle stillness before the red warfare of the sun, and birds would burst through the ligatures of the pirate's remarkable burden-gnarled leg of sculpted wood, and there was no language available to convey the tranquillity, the suction between event and consequence.

It was during this time that I finally found my carbuncular heart expanding to welcome Scotland's purgatoried beauty, its unaffectionate familiarity. It was purely a weird country, overwhelmed by the fertility of its wildness, its originality, but I could sit like the stoic heron and watch swallows of medallion white burrow into my blind friend's leg before erupting from his kneecap in gold-fledged song without me feeling a pensive or feeble desire to know anything greater. Here was a country as energetic, brazen, popeyed, unforeseeable and authentic as a fevered Italian ally. There was some part of me that Scotland had to break before it could repair me with its true immensity. I wasn't avoiding to recall my losses, but I'd sure gained something. I believe the whispered commodity is "insight", but to be honest I think the sweetest mystery is how I awoke one morning and discovered that I possessed a love for birds. Which maybe I had to encounter, to taste, to claim as my own in order to justify the few events that follow:

When I'd survived the month's adverse labour, working my cuticles into my eyeballs to keep awake while the whole optic fibre of my being ached from the physical trauma of our annihilating moating regimen – sometimes enduring forty-eight hours of consecutive work, broken by forty-eight hours of sleep and gasping recovery – I experienced a moment of unbiased grace on the day that the final clod of soil was hewn from the hand-wrangled canal. I collapsed in our moat, this singularity which we had wrought, my shirt fantailed around my forehead and my perfidious suede shoes hanging, in a travesty of elegance, from the end-heft of my shovel. My feet were burning, toes webbed in topsoil and bog strata, and my neck was stricken by a wine-stain rash of defeat beneath the glower of the Scottish sun. It reminded me of a bulldog who'd suffered a kick in the balls too many, did the sun. So I clenched my eyelids against the malign threat of evil heat and soon I felt a

114

wetness engulf my left foot, transforming the tissue of mud and moss grafted between my exhausted piggy-wiggies into a black sediment of clay.

Padraig had finagled a complex, convoluted and impressive pulley system from a nearby grazing loch so that water flowed with lustre and vibrance, as fatally sublime as an avalanche, into the network of aqueduct-like access chutes that bristled from the contours of our moat. The ditch was now concentrating the passage of the water with barbarous efficiency, so that before I could discern the theoretically nimble course of action, I was stunned from my reverie by a flume of centrifugal, bracing mad streamwater that pitched me onto my face into the naked earth, and then beneath a numbing cobalt undertow of moat silt.

The water had claimed me, and now, exanimate from bloodyminded toil, I was floundering beneath the aggravated, rippling surface! I ate constellations of wheeling, oil-viscous, scorched whirlpools of muck, breathed it in, drew the slime at the bottom of the culvert down to the bottom of my thrashing lungs. I sought air, I scoured for the breakspace, I sent my nostrils in a stutter for the surface. Dirt burned between teeth. My brain defibrillated, lost traction, abandoned clarity, submitted to the fireworks display of the nearly-slain. I collided against the bank, dismantling my ribcage. The whole while I caught flashes of colour, a scintillating exhibition, between breaths as I drowned.

Where was Padraig Dunlap, my fractured saint? I could hear the pirate drone like a raven above the undertow. He commanded a reckoning of sun-warped dwarven bravery through the blur and morphology of colours and the quickened slapping of the charged foam of the canal: his fierce form crested above me, reviling the sky. Two hands broke into my domain, pumping the channel of ditch-water for purchase until his questing fingers located my right nostril. Knuckles assailed my septum, thumbnails loosened my eye sockets. For a panicked interlude I could not be certain if I was being drowned or saved – there is a vocational overlap between so many diametrically-opposed acts and sometimes it seems a marvel we even disentangle them at all – but then I felt the surface receding and I was squirting out sabres of snot and bile and streamwater, purging shit from my lungs with accusatory, banal, luxurious breaths, my

115

chest thrumming and my throat farming out injured gasps to the peeping greenery.

Padraig hunched over the moat, disconcerting me with a brittle sneer. He tugged at his beard, as if announcing the approach of an oncoming train. I languished, strangled by running water, on the embankment of the moat, out of my mind with celestial exhaustion.

I bided my time to regain my thread of depleted sanity, rolling my jaw in a lazy arc to emulate a dog that'd been stung in the mouth. Language soon followed, in spurts of haggard rancour.

'Why the fuck did it take you so long to react? I could've been resurfacing in five more minutes as a makeshift raft with graveyard flesh. I beg pardon, because I'm grateful that you even assaulted my nasal passages to wrangle me onto the bank at all: but Chrissakes, Padraig, any longer and the only activity that would be occurring in my nostrils within days would be the microscopic tour being conducted by an autopsy camera to confirm cause of death.' I sneezed, squeezing out a sleeve of run-off, and my teeth chattered.

The pirate shrugged with a nonplussed leisure, his smile rippling through his head. 'I s'pose the obvious wouldn't signify a sufficient answer,' he muttered, nodding his thumb at the churning moat. 'It's not inhuman of me to feel inertia at the appearance of such unequalled brilliance, I'd contend. I mean, some products of direct sensation just demand a reasonable and uncertain awe.'

I didn't buy this – defending one's dangerous neglect by claiming such egotism was a reaction to the miraculous – if only because there was nothing *breathtaking* about our sweat-trammelled imperfect moat, not least to justify a failure to act at the prospect of a possible murder, and I could sense resentment clogging in my craw. Yet I quelled my venom and indulged the pirate's condescending eye by wearily propping myself up, chest consumed by fire, to gaze with a jaded affection at the causeway, and then I saw the serene theatre feted before my yawning eyes.

There were swans on the moat! – red swans, *Cygnus toro*, impossible birds, phantasmagoric gentry, a flotilla of streamlined craft stencilled into sunshine, seventeen creatures as alien as a fantasy palimpsesting into the present, *like finding lobsters living on the moon*. My eyelids bulged with tears. I could not fully understand their meaning and place. The tiger swans encircled us, displacing surplus water over the bank, gliding like gilded fruit on the grade of the causeway, a motorcade of birds as grand as pimp limousines. I'd never discounted the authenticity of Adolfo's assertions, but there was something inconceivable about the proof, something similar to earning love.

How severe their elegance! Their plumage retained the blood of the Pentecost, it caught the light in a dizzy of overexposed photo brights. I brimmed with sorrow and a lingering drunk, soaring off the ignited marvel of their lazy circus. I fumbled with my mobile phone, erratic, teeming with fear, the terror that something so spontaneous and fleeting in its grace would end, and I toggled to my pixel camera fast enough to confuse my fingers. I thrust the camera to my eyes, cradling the mobile aloft, and I seized one artful snapshot.

The birds heard the mechanism whir, and charged into the air in a volted fever of thrashing wingspans, their accusatory calls sounding like elk separated by pine forest. They wuthered *en masse*, staging a tournament of weaponised yelps, as their seraphic forms scaled the violet peaks of unpeopled sky. Each one was probably too incendiary for this leaky ecosystem, less an extinct dearth of a regretted species of bird and more similar to tortured perfections, like champion greyhounds or beautiful burns victims. You could not dispute your eyes, for all those varlets of the wing flickered into the glare of the day before retreating to the wides at the bank of the planet, reminding me of the silver people on a lost cinema, playing for the monkeys and ferns in a sprawling jungle. I felt like I'd intruded on a movie I'd never seen, and the jaws of the flytraps were clapping in the narrows of light.

I could do little but sit, squinting into the sun, trying to recover my scarce mental clarity while I shrunk at the finale to that matinee study of my dead friend's righteous vision. I held a phone, displaying a genius photograph, in my wet mitts. It would've been worthy of Cézanne, this throbbing echo of reds, if not for the thumbpad squeezed into the far right corner of the frame.

✭

I am a moat-maker. How I came to be a moat-maker (which was not my intended profession, for I fancied one day that I might lecture

117

other listless dilettantes on the empirical significance of bog deaths in the forgotten swamps of English academia), how I was witness to the demise of my widest friend – wide, for he once possessed a gasping heart of thoroughbred renown – and how this all conspired to befall me in Scotland, where women are on first-name basis with the fungus that spawns on their ceilings, has little to do with the debris of my last fractured romance, and more to do with the legend of a swan, a disastrous letter, and a last-minute ploy to ensnare an unsung wolf-like terror.

It all devolved into a poetic and taut conclusion, with blood flowing ferrous and five ways, when the pirate sporting his sinful limbs escorted the full complement of his livestock through the arches of our moat-walled bodega.

I followed with bristling hands, hooting and stamping to ensure all sheep and malformed cattle wended their kind through the muster of green fog, their mottled and birth-merled coats summoning atlases of martian terrain between folds of supple bone. The exodus carved its passage, reaping a disenchanting fen-stench of pearled shit as it proceeded. We stamped our boots and hollered our fighting anthem. The sheep brayed in a tongue reserved in secret for fleecy freaks, roving their panicked galvanic eyes at my bared teeth, disserviced by the wet parp of their leaking bowels.

Their fear would soon be authenticated. The foresight of a common sheep of the highlands is an instrument of abrasive limits; it knows of no threat unplanned. We kept trudging through the muck, human cur of the Kilmarnock steppe. Some irascible veterans of the black-masked sheep clan sought to discredit our largesse and repeated command, but there's only so many occasions that a surly old ewe can withstand impact on its hindquarters by a wooden beam fastened to its one-eyed master's pelvis before it must, by consequence, relent from exhibiting a maverick sense of independence. We were hectored at by a few begrudging bleats before the entire convoy had ensconced itself behind the stone promontory, and within seconds of their vexed, snout-champing arrival, the procession quelled its complaints. We were dismissed with an ornery snort, and soon the livestock was concerning itself with the buffet of coarse sweetgrass and thistle sprouting from within their annexe.

Padraig and I careened against the comforting contours of the archway stone, perilously near weary collapse, and we shared a smoke between ourselves, my last cigarette from the case crumpled into my arse-pocket. I smiled, an abstraction of change in a dustbowl of our making with carcinogens roaming the polyps of my accelerating brain. It was a fine day, gold like copperplate around the edges. A single red swan wheeled lazily on the surface of our foaming canal, like a Chinese paper boat. We set to work.

We wired the dismantled clatter of Vasquez Duchamp's chalky remains from skull to shinbone, approaching the task with the meticulous eye of a professional clockmaker, labouring over those brittle ligatures until a man of wire and decay formed beneath us. The skeleton was in absolute form, a transparent gentleman composed from broken parts, and he was so light and untroubling to move that when we transferred Vasquez to our stake, affixing the apparition to the totem with yards of naval rope until he was held fast, it was startling to discover that he commanded attention like the best society of scarecrow.

Padraig drenched the inert sentinel with a blast of blood, milk, meat and fishgut. Vasquez strobed like a lamp, flickered from all-white to all-red in one foul discharge of Padraig Dunlap's bucket of chumming slurry. He dripped between layers of petals and carnage. Our hand-wrangled chasm was stockpiled with serrated blades, enclosed with its latticed grate, and lorded over by a fat, royal shark's heart: purple like the contents of a baked blueberry pie. Our skeletal guardian grinned at us from its outpost, amassed in a coat of attractive murder. We waited in the moonlight, from the parapet of the stone annexe, our faces tangled with bloodlust as the wind cradled the tang of fish carrion over the sleeping bayside slopes. We panted between our teeth and watched for the monstrous sign of the Ayrshire Lobo.

At about 2:00am, when we had both peevishly succumbed to sleep, there resounded screams that throttled my numb, slow reflexes. I lurched to my feet, breath a wreck through my whistling nose, and I braved into the night's smouldering mass, clutching my spiral of flame – a torch brazier – to my person as though I emerged to convey the most ancient words of the serious, dark Good Book. I defied the policy of blindness: I came with the stealth of glass feet, my fangs breaking through the boast of my English calm. I was here to kill that creature, with violent economy, and avenge the damaged flight of my ravaged spiritual brother. I crowed with a caballed madness, and descended amidst the slumped, harassed forms of the sheep with my breath swelling in my ears.

Just out of earshot, I caught the refrain of aborted screams from out beyond the moat. Bricktop was shrieking the stars out of the sky. I could smell a grotesque mixture of canine impurity and sweating flesh, and some vacant chamber within my chest very quickly heaved with the terrific weight of regret. I called out to Padraig, again and again, until my throat burned from the urgency.

✠

The protean lustre of the morning railed at me to survey the *danse macabre* of the previous night, and will my brain into processing the assault with tender dismay. The Lobo had thwarted our trap, feasted on the last relics of Vasquez Duchamp's ivory spectre, thrust Bricktop into a hysterical seizure, and grappled with Padraig Dunlap – the final member of a refined and mythopoeic heritage of adventurer – out on the moors with the wrath of a lion confronting an unflagging Rutger Hauer with cyborg offcuts.

It had been one dojo ponytail shy of a *Highlander* episode, and now the ruination remained strewn at my feet while the daylight cast offensive aspersions on my sunken tourist features. I clenched my eyelids against the intrusion of private oxyacetylene sunshine. My toes dangled in the milieu of withered balloons above the suck of the sorry, jade causeway. The sheep were content to occupy themselves with the standard mystery of a new, plenteous breakfast. It was an hour of reverence, to sit in disrepair by the moat and bawl your glands dry of wealth.

I cried so hard my head rang from the constant liquid purge. I harboured an ache to hear the pirate's inventive and wharf-bustled tones vibrate from the mire of the land. I could just about die from the untended appetite. After exhausting my stamina for ostentatious misery, I freshened my face with a splash of moat-water and harassed my hair into a functional part.

120

It took me a wheeze through the teeth and a self-directed threat to my continued wellbeing to muster the ignorant gumption to peer into the pit beneath the damage of the naked stake and the fractured, latticed grate. I had to wedge my toe into the chasm and level off the grille before the potential aftermath of last night's barbarism became apparent. I narrowed my eyes as I've seen peregrine falcons practice, and I allowed myself to suffer whatever said trough of trauma presented me with, resolved to confront the extinction of my mentor in the art of the labour-intensive moat.

Something like an aluminium boomerang caught and refracted the sunlight at the base of the pit, mangled and misshapen between the thresh of converging blades. I squinted, no longer dignified in the manufacture of tears, demanding discipline from my stinging, orange orbs. Gradually my vision adjusted and my blood cooled. It necessitated ten minutes of early-morning toil, but I soon succeeded in lassoing the incongruous artefact with the looped end of a winch-rope and the sun-glanced instrument came hurtling out of the dark towards me.

I heaved, applying my shoulders to the rodeo arithmetic of the moment, and after retreating ten metres I was able to haul the object clear of the knife-arrayed obstruction. There it was, a symbol severed from its signifier: Padraig Dunlap's metal arm lay like a twenty-third-century shrimp in a cluster of alloy ligaments.

It was time for me to return home, lest I foster ruination within everything I claimed of value. I readied myself for the return journey, casting my gaze over the plateau for that cowardly chimpanzee. Scotland was almost certainly dead to me now. I would not recover any future opportunity to win back the destruction of the day. I rotated to discover something vibrating beneath my suede: I was invariably certain that it was the dwindling vehicle of a dying locust, and my heel was about to descend to exact that apologetic, stalk-quashed crunch when I felt the sudden formidable *absence* in my jeans where my phone commonly clustered. Again, the abandoned phone trembled in the tall grass! Out in the marshes of yore, where eldritch beasts of cryptozoological repute roamed the highland trespasses, and here someone within the schema of my current reality was striving to fucking call me! I bolted to my knees and slapped the receiver to my jaw.

'Hello? Sebastian Fenugreek Sackworth on the blower.'

Ísleifur Reykjavík's voice ascended from the vacant green perfidy of my surrounds. I'd forgotten that the Icelander had retained my number. 'Sebastian, I'm assuming you remember the Icelandic recluse who bestowed the funky monkey on your person? Of course, if you encounter any difficulties, I feel no momentary anguish to affect my famous mid-west American drawl if you require a clue. I can even discharge my shotgun into the distance should the need for subsequent clarification arise.'

I swallowed, and began navigating my way towards my sprawl of neglected camp supplies, yesterday's breakfast plates radiating day beneath the unflappable skies.

'Oho, if it isn't his honour, the heir to the Bay of Smoke. Look, don't play daft, Ísleifur. I don't know how to frame the consequences of last night's preoccupations, but the shit has hit the rotor, here, in East Ayrshire. I would recommend that you steel yourself and prepare for some galling, difficult news.'

'You refer, of course, to Padraig Dunlap's death. Am I correct in my deduction?' The Icelander, even despite eschewing most emotional complications, appeared to be uncannily resolute about something so fresh and rapacious, and I had little time to discern how he knew what I had only minutes previous come to terms with. 'That's why I'm calling, Sebastian. They've recovered his body – the Edinburgh homicide department. It's already being declaimed to the world on local radio.'

I felt my waning reserves of energy dissipate with each slowing footfall. I croaked, a dinosaur not devised for this exile. 'Where'd they find it, Ísleifur?'

'On the coast. The shoreline skirting the Irvine Bar Channel, to be exact. Apparently a few beach-combing locals claim to have unearthed the remains beside the channel this morning, at sunup, before contacting the local Strathclyde constabulary. It's made for intense morning speculation.'

'Sorry, I may be somewhat deficient of the total complement of my faculties here, but I believe you just advised that Padraig's body was *unearthed* this morning? Unearthed from sodding *what*?'

'The fucking Lobo, Sebastian! This inquisitive coterie of wee seaside gypsies stumbled upon the carcass of our giant hyena, territorialised by a swarm of blowflies, down there on the sodding *sand verge*. These are Scottish folk, Sebastian, so they foresaw no harm in probing the violated creature with an armoury of investigative sticks. Mad fuckers, I tell you. Anyway, that's how they recovered Padraig's body – they had to exhume the remains from inside the Lobo's abdomen. I'm not kidding, there are apparently photojournalists and biologists descending in packs to the site as we exalt over this quaint little chat.'

'Does it sound like I'm exalting?' I transferred the mobile to my other ear, and gnawed at the plump muscle of my tongue for an instant. 'So that's it? They've stumbled onto the remnants of Scotland's largest warm-blooded predator?'

'The way I heard it, the Lobo had combusted – that is to say, exploded – by shitting out its guts in an attempt to digest our mutual friend.'

I clapped a palm over my eyelids, overwhelmed by the violence of the unstable animal kingdom. 'You're really painting a picture here, Ísleifur. My gratitude for the veracity of your talent.'

'That's not the least of it: they'll be wanting to conduct an interview with you, clarify your personal involvement in confronting the Lobo the night before its kingly ilk dissolved into mere BBC speculation. You did have a hand in this, didn't you? You *were* with Padraig when he reasoned it as a feasible gambit to attack a monster of carnivorous prowess, weren't you?' The Icelander paused, and I assumed he interpreted my knackered sigh as a slip of complicity. 'You'll probably be paid for this, Sebastian. You do understand this? The repercussions of all this deathly extravagance will be unequivocally lucrative.'

I hiccupped, temporarily perplexed. 'I say, what's all this rubbish about exposure and payment? I'm heartbroken, here. I'm English, I'm emotionally-depleted, and I'm an anthropology alumnus. The rest is all bollocks and arseholes.'

'I also need to explain that you received a letter, Sebastian. Actually, two paper communiqués to be precise. At the hostel, to the room you were occupying before you left to seek employment from our man who was swallowed whole.'

'What letter? Who are they from? What do they concern?' I swallowed a whole stockpile of stomach bile.

'One's from the scholarship board at the University of Kent. They're retracting your PhD bursarship on grounds of research evasion. They stipulate that you've submitted no documentation to testify to your progress, and suggest that if you were to appeal the allegation you would have to contend with not acquiring ethical clearance before departing for Scotland.'

I could just about fathom a future entirely devoted to foetal-positioned catatonia. 'Ísleifur, why the fuck are you reading my mail?'

'The other's from the Italian executrix of the estate for one Adolfo Luisa Cavaggio, Esq. He's bequeathed his inheritance to you.' The Icelander chuckled, a quizzical gesture of allegiance, and cleared his throat. 'He's left you almost everything.'

I grunted voluntarily, and oscillated with the exasperated grace of a weathervane. 'Do you know something? After everything, I still captured a photograph of *Cygnus toro*, Ísleifur.'

This shut the Icelander up. We were both as silent as cosmonaut chimpanzees orbiting one another within an interspatial vacuum. Eventually the Icelander hissed, "You'll be famous", and I could then permit myself to bask in the intensity of his envy with immediate confidence.

'You'll need to personally sign for Adolfo's estate so your bequest can be processed. Where are you now?'

I wasn't sure. Somewhere beyond the ken of mortal reckoning, I hazarded. 'Look, I'll have to call you back, there's someone I need to reach because if I don't risk the venture right now, I'll never possess the belly-fire to try my hand.'

I severed the call and began toggling through the screed of names archived in my mobile's contact list. I was perspiring, my hand was quaking in the still clasp of morning. I saw the two names, pulsing before me one after the other: PAMELA REDDING, and just as resonant in that crepuscular glow of autumn, PER HAVEN. The air stank of pollen. I stood adrift for the longest minute of my life, and heard just beyond the horizon the squall of fighting gulls plunging for sand dollars as the waves scorned each choice I cast as my own. Bricktop was back amidst the foliage of his beech tree and he was labouring over the Rubik's Cube with his own style of gallant moral adversity.

124

'What the fuck,' I muttered, somehow happier than I knew how to tolerate, and pressed dial. 'Hey, it's Sebastian. You won't believe this, svelte pins,' I rehearsed, waiting for the pips to break. 'I am a moat-maker.'

From there, I had to suppose that I would find the words.

Kirk Marshall is an award-winning Australian writer, and teacher of English Literature and Media (Film & T.V. Studies) at RMIT University. He is the author of *The Signatory* (Skylight Press; 2012), *Carnivalesque, And: Other Stories* (Black Rider Press; 2011), and *A Solution to Economic Depression in Little Tokyo, 1953.* He edits *Red Leaves* / 紅葉, the English-language/Japanese bi-lingual literary journal. He now suffers migraines in two languages.